MW01713000

Also by David Gilmour

Back On Tuesday
How Boys See Girls

An Affair with the Moon

An Affair with the Moon

David Gilmour

Random House of Canada
Toronto New York London Sydney Auckland

Published in Canada in 1993 by Random House of Canada Limited, Toronto.

Canadian Cataloguing in Publication Data

Gilmour, David, 1949-

An affair with the moon

ISBN 0-394-22360-8

I. Title.

PS856.I56A75 1993 C813'.54 C93-094046-8

PR9199.3.G55A75 1993

Cover illustration: Blair Drawson

Printed and bound in Canada

10 9 8 7 6 5 4 3 2 1

For Sarah Teskey
with love

Chapter One

It was autumn now, those honey-soft days in late September, and I woke up feeling queasy with nostalgia. All day long it tugged at me. Around three, I gave in to it and wandered back to my old university campus. No one recognized me. Three athletic boys, stripped to the waist, threw a football back and forth on a sun-dappled lawn. A girl read Chaucer under an oak tree. Another girl, dressed in green, sat cross-legged on the grass, her eyes shut, her pale face turned up into the sun. A boy in a fedora crossed the lawn. He had the face of a child, that hat must have been his dad's.

I went into a pink building, down a circular flight of stairs and into the cafeteria. I saw a clear, almost hallucinatorily vivid picture of Harrow rushing in almost twenty years ago, a scarf around his neck even in summer, a worn sports jacket with patched elbows, and those wild globular eyes–they were so excited, so full of life and humour and appetite. He was an unstoppable young boy. He'd been on my mind a lot these days. It was fall and I always thought about him in the fall.

I ran into a girl who worked at my neighbourhood video store. At first we had trouble placing each other. The context was all wrong. But then it clicked into place. She was starting college, it was her third day. She spoke tentatively, politely, as if I were the school principal and she didn't want to detain me. Her friend, who had a long, aquiline nose, looked up at me and smiled nervously. They were both very short. She was studying commerce and English and fine art.

"A balanced diet," I said, sounding rather old, rather stuffy, like an elder statesman.

I got myself a coffee; a woman in a green smock gave it to me in a white styrofoam cup. I asked her where the mugs were. She was from eastern Europe and didn't understand the word.

"Cups," I said. I made a gesture with my hand.

"Gone," she said cheerfully.

I sat at a small table along the wall. Two pretty girls in tank tops came in. They poured themselves a coffee each and then filed over to the cream and sugar stand. There was much fussing, giggling, and they seemed to take forever putting the sugar in their cups. We all watched them, watched their summer-tanned backs. One was heavier than the other but they were well suited for each other; they were new friends, they'd just met, I guessed, in residence. They took so long putting the cream in their coffee I was tempted to say something, but I didn't. I was afraid they'd think I was using that as a pretext to talk to them, to pick them up. And they'd be right of course.

In a while, the tables around me cleared and I was left alone. There was no one, not even ghosts. I pulled out Harrow's letter. It was in a worn blue envelope, covered in bright stamps. It smelt of the sea, of foreign places, of excitement. I'd been saving it all day, waiting for just the right moment, the right place to read it.

Dear Christian,
Rio didn't work out. In fact it turned out to be a worse idea than doing drugs with a psychotic in a house full of guns. (Sorry. I haven't had much company. I must be getting punchy.)But listen: about that last letter. Don't take it too seriously. I was in my cups and feeling a little sorrowful. The truth is, if I had to do it over, I'd plug him again.

I'm staying in a strange little hotel. Last night, I saw a message for Jean-Paul Sartre on the lobby desk. But the sunsets here - with the long boats moving up the river, and the river all silver from the sun - it's heartbreaking, absolutely heartbreaking.

I have such violent dreams at night. It must be the medication.

I miss you and love you - even though you fucked me. Just kidding.

Harrow

P.S. What does *one do in the tropics? Wait for dinner, pick at your skin and something else. I forget.*

Chapter Two

There was a knock at the door of our classroom and a new kid came in. He was frowning and smiling, he looked a bit crazy, a little boy constantly guessing how he ought to seem.

"I'm Harrow," he said and laughed.

They sat him near me. I watched him carefully. He had bulging eyes, a ruffle of wild blond hair and exaggerated mannerisms. He clapped his hands when he laughed; he frowned when he listened. Everyone took to him, they watched him with anticipation, like children ready to play. I saw it happen all day long. Even the teacher called him Harrow. They never did that. They never called you by your first name.

After school, when the 4:35 bell rang, I pushed my way through a group of students. One of them had a donut stain on his blazer.

"How come everyone calls you Harrow?" I said.

He turned two big, shiny eyes at me.

"Because that's my name."

Later that evening, I was sitting on the front steps of my house. It was after dinner; a gold light fell across the street. I had the family cat in my lap and she was purring. Suddenly a boy on a green bicycle rode up. It was Harrow Winncup. He had a brown sack over his shoulder. Something heavy was inside it.

"Come on," he said.

"Where are you going?"

"Down to the lake shore."

"My parents don't let me go down there."

He shrugged. The cat wiggled in my lap.

"What've you got in the bag?"

"It's a secret," he said.

I put down the cat and went down the driveway and got my bicycle.

"I'm going to the park," I said to mother.

We got on our bikes and we rode down through the brown city. It was fall, just getting dark. You could smell it in the streets, that exciting, thrilling smell of fall. Even back then it made me nostalgic, even when I had hardly anything to remember.

By the time we got to the train yards it was dark. We rode over a bridge and came to a stop at the foot of a tall rusted water tower. Harrow leaned his bike against a pole. He stood at the bottom and looked up. The street lights came on. The stars came out. The moon rose. You could smell water on the other side of the railway lines.

"Come on," he said and then he started up the ladder with his sack. We climbed and climbed, hand over hand, the city fell away below us, you could feel the breeze pulling at your pants. We climbed up and up, Harrow holding the bag over his shoulder. Finally we got to the top. I scrunched in beside him. We stood there for a moment, our legs shaking with the strain. From up there, I could see the whole city, I could see an amusement park, I could see the red lights of Chinatown, the tower of our school like a moon in a child's book. Out in the harbour a coal boat sat in the middle of the black lake, a green light blinking on its starboard side.

Then, bracing himself against the ladder, Harrow hoisted up the bag. I peeked inside.

"It's a television tube," he said. "I found it behind a store."

He worked it toward the mouth of the bag, laughing with the effort. Then it came free. I saw something glimmer in the moonlight for just a second and then it fell way into the darkness, falling down into the giant empty rusted cup. There was silence and then a terrible roar, a thunder like the end of the world, a boom that shook the sides of the water tank. It roared up out of the blackness, its breath blew against our faces. Its size terrified me, like a train, like a volcano, like God. I could see Harrow. His shoulders shook, tears ran down his eyes, laughter twisted his mouth into a grimace.

"Implosion," he said.

From the first day, I had an awful crush on him. I say crush because when I decided to write this book, I tried to think of a whole lot of wonderful things he'd done; but the truth is I couldn't think of that much. So it must have been a crush, the kind you get on boys when you're little, a kind of aura they carry about with them that quite transforms the spot they stand on, the things they touch, the clothes they wear, into the centre of the universe.

He came from a small northern town and moved in down the street from me. It was a great brown brick house; three storeys tall, like a castle. And in the morning, around 8:30, I'd stand under his window and holler up at him and the window would fly open and a blond curly-haired boy burst out the window with a cry and then he'd dash downstairs and we'd head off to school, up Dunvegan Road right to the top of the hill where the whole city lay out before us.

I never had as good a friend again. And now, I know, I never will. After a certain age, that stuff never happens again.

I remember once, in grade ten, a teacher read us Shakespeare's Sonnet 30 and sent us home to study it for a test. It was the first time I was ever moved by poetry and when I got to those two last lines, the ones that go

But if the while I think on thee, dear friend,
All losses are restored and sorrows end.

I felt my throat catch, I thought about my friend Harrow. Up there in my yellow study, where my parents sent me to do my homework, I paced the floor and imagined heroic deeds, scaling a castle wall, duelling with a villain, things I might do to prove the depth of my friendship. It was quite feverish, I suppose.

I never understood, even as a child, why I wasn't more popular. Sometimes I longed to stop a boy in the hall, a boy who was surrounded by chattering friends, I wanted to stop him and say, "Honestly, you can take my word for it, I'm much more interesting than these people. And I'll come to a better end too. You'll see."

But I was too shy and my shyness, I think, took on the appearance of arrogance, of coldness. Once I got to know people, I was fine. But I needed an entrée; and Harrow gave it to me. When I was with Harrow, I hid, so to speak, in the shadow of his noisy, gregarious personality for those first crucial moments, until I could get my footing and say something.

Even as a child he gave things and places a sense of occasion, long before either of us knew what the words meant. I remember once, a couple of years after he moved into the neighbourhood, we were playing spin the bottle with a couple of young, freckled girls. We were fourteen then, and at one point, I can't remember why, Harrow withdrew from the game leaving me and the two girls. As I reached greedily for the bottle, I heard one of them say, the pretty one, "It's no fun without Harrow," and she brushed off her skirt and rose quickly to her feet. Of course it was a devastating moment, my face flushed hot and I didn't dare raise my eyes off the bottle. I remember it almost thirty years later. But in a peculiar way I sort of understood what she meant. I never understood it, never understood why that halo didn't float over my own head, but it didn't. Yet I recognized it when I saw it over someone else's.

Perhaps I'm giving him too much credit. Perhaps the pretty girl simply didn't want me kissing her. Who knows?

And his mother? Well, she was something else. I knew she was trouble the first time I laid eyes on her. A cold, smiling bitch with a green emerald ring on her finger. I'm older now, I should have forgiven her, but I haven't. I'd like to dig her up and give her a kick.

For a while there I was the cat's pyjamas in the Winncup household. His mother loved me. She was like an animal that way, she knew that my mother could do things for her, get her into the right clubs, introduce her to the right crowd.

I stayed overnight on weekends. I flew in his father's seaplane, I did "the honours" at Winncup parties. I liked doing that. It meant you put on a blazer, flannels, a school tie, and had dinner in the kitchen amidst all the anticipation: the maids scurrying back and forth with sandwich trays, caterers coming in the back door with turkeys and soups, a bartender putting on his white jacket in the maid's room. And then, around nine, when the party started, Harrow and I came downstairs; we waded carefully through the perfume and cigar smoke and the guests, serving tea or refreshing drinks. It was a chance to show off, to show your good manners, how clever you were, and it made my mother very happy.

But when I was fifteen, I got drunk with Harrow in his basement; I got drunk on warm scotch and I was doing an imitation of his mother. I had my hands held together and was speaking in a fake, syrupy voice, my head crooked to the side with a pained expression on my face. Suddenly, the door ripped open and Florence Winncup stepped briskly across the threshhold and clasped her white fingers around my neck.

"Mother," Harrow said.

She took a step backward, frowned, then quite incongruously, smiled.

"It's time to go home, Christian," she said.

I hurried from the room and up the stairs but I was wildly drunk, my feet slipped from under me and I landed with a crash. I heard Harrow laugh.

"It's not funny, Harrow," his mother said. But the fury was gone; it seemed forced now, held-onto. It'll be all right, I thought as I staggered down the street; tomorrow, it'll all be all right. But it wasn't.

After that, I wasn't the golden boy anymore.

I think it was kind of a heartbreak for my mother.

And then came the party.

It was early fall, a foggy Hallowe'en night. My parents had just come home after a party. I heard them come in downstairs, I heard my father slam the door, shaking the beams in the house; he did it last thing every night, he thought it was the only way to make sure it was properly locked.

Then some time later, after I had drifted back down to sleep, I heard my door open and the sound of beads clicking together. It was my mother's blue dress. The sound came near me. I could smell cigarette smoke and liquor. She sat down at the end of the bed and for a long while said nothing. I lifted my head off the pillow.

"Hi," I said.

She was, to use her words, a little squiffy. I heard it in her voice, in the misplaced emphasis on the words to make them sound normal.

"How was the party?" I asked.

"Fine," she said. There was a pause. I knew something else was coming.

"But I'm not going to see Florence Winncup anymore."

Something cold ran through me. I was wide awake now, although I pretended not to be.

"Why not?" I asked.

"Because there was another boy there tonight, doing the honours."

"Who was it?" I asked in a strange voice.

"It was Tommy Murphy."

I felt a sudden weight on my chest.

"Mom," I said. "Harrow probably felt sorry for him. He's got such terrible skin, he practically never goes to parties."

I could tell she was turning it over in her mind.

"Do you think so?" she said. It broke my heart to hear her say that.

"I'm sure of it."

"Maybe," she said.

She bent over and kissed me on the cheek.

"I probably smell awful," she said.

"No, not at all."

I felt her weight leave the bed. The door opened, a pencil of light crossed my bed. Then it was gone.

After that, I had to sneak around to see Harrow; like a teen romance, Romeo and Juliet. Had to wait at the end of the street for him. Some nights, I'd wait until after midnight and then I'd tiptoe out and I'd go over to his house and throw a stone up at his window and he'd creep down the maid's stairs and meet me around the back in the lilac-scented garden and we'd head off into the city together. We'd go to the Village, we'd go to a coffee house and look at the beautiful girls with long black hair and pale faces.

Sometimes I'd say is your mom still mad about that drinking and Harrow would kind of wrinkle up his brow, the way he always did when he was uncomfortable and say, yeah, sort of. But it'll pass.

And I'd sort of swallow it. I wanted to ask him why he didn't stick up for me, you know, insist. But I was afraid to. I was afraid of Harrow getting mad at me, afraid of him not liking me anymore, of him dropping me like, say, Donny Temple, this other guy at school.

We went skating once. It was in the middle of the night, snow piled up in ghostly banks. We skated in silence, just the sound of our blades on the dry ice. Harrow was a natural athlete but for some reason, even though he came from the deep north, he wasn't a good skater. He couldn't turn left and I think it sort of bugged him. So that night, he was practising, taking these choppy little steps, around and around in a tight circle.

I wasn't a good skater either. I had weak ankles but I could swing left. I could really fly. With my hands behind my back, taking long graceful strides, I swooped around the rink, screeching to a halt near him. Overcome by excitement and the night air, I couldn't help myself.

"Take bigger steps!" I hollered. "Take bigger steps! Like me!"

At first I didn't think he heard me. So I skated a little closer and hollered it again.

"Take bigger steps!"

He turned on me. "Don't tell me how to skate," he snapped. It had the shock of a sudden animal bite. I could feel my behind contract like I was going to poo in my pants. I laughed wildly, it was nerves, and I said no, no, I wasn't trying to teach you how to skate, I was just ... and then I couldn't think of anything else to add. The sentence just came to a halt and he skated away to the other end of the rink and left me standing there, all jammed up, like an old typewriter.

So you see what I mean. I was pretty scared of him.

One day he came up to me in front of the tuck shop; it was after school, a grey, cloudy, lonely day. He looked very grim.

"I'm going to Jamaica," he said. "We're going on holiday."

I looked away. "Oh."

There was a pause. At the end of the driveway a white car pulled into the headmaster's driveway. I looked quickly, more like a peek, at Harrow. He was still looking at me, he was frowning, waiting for the right moment.

"I'm taking Tommy Murphy with me," he said. It winded me, it landed like a heavy wooden spear right into the solar plexus. I was afraid to look at him, afraid he'd see it on my face, but he kept looking at me anyway, his face dark, worried, which added to the humiliation.

I opened my mouth; nothing came out. And then I walked home, very quickly, the street, the brown houses, the melting snow whipped by me like dirty sheets. I went straight up to my room and I closed the door and I sat by the window on my blue bed, staring out at the big tree in the backyard. Then I heard my mother's voice.

"Christian, are you home? Is that you?"

She came into my room. She looked at my face, then she got very serious.

"Did something happen with Harrow?"

I told her about Tommy Murphy.

"I'm going to kill that woman," she said.

While they were away, while they collected sea shells and ran wild like savages on the white sand, I went skating at the rink. I went there on a Sunday afternoon; the ice was soft and earth showed through in patches; no one was there except for a father and his little boy, who kept falling over. I skated around and around and around, the afternoon went on forever.

Finally I ran way from home. I was fifteen. My father had a nervous breakdown and sold our house and they put me in boarding school and moved away from the city. It was a bad mistake; it was the end of our family. Within six months my father was dead, my mother living in Mexico. But before that happened, when they told me I was going to boarding school, I sat down with my mother at the kitchen table and I said, I'll run away if you put me in boarding. And she said, I have no choice, we can't afford to live here anymore.

And they put me in boarding and three weeks later, in the middle of the night, I packed a suitcase and stole out of the school and took a taxi over to Harrow's house and threw a stone up at his window. A few minutes later he joined me in the garden.

“Here,” he said. He gave me eleven dollars. “If you stay away longer than three days, you can keep it.”

Three weeks later, I telephoned him from Mexico. I was staying with an retired newspaper man from New York.

“You’re famous,” Harrow whispered into the phone. “Now everyone wants to run away. They caught one of the boarders last night. He said he was pulling a Christian.”

Then I phoned my mother. I’d had enough, I wanted to come home; she sent me plane fare. I saw Harrow my first night back. We had a coffee in a Chinese restaurant.

“I slept with a woman,” I said. “She had a patch over one eye.”

“Oh yeah?” Harrow said, fascinated. “Did she take that off too?”

They let me back in school but I was too far gone and I got expelled at the end of the year. Not invited back was how my mother phrased it. I went to an experimental school for rich, disturbed kids. It was up north, the classes ended at noon, we could smoke cigarettes and grow our hair. I didn’t see Harrow, hardly at all, that year, but it was all right. I fancied he was a little jealous about my new school. Maybe not, maybe that’s absurd. In fact even writing the sentence makes me see Harrow’s face, it’s a look of flat dismay, a kind of unspoken come-off-it. But I know one thing. It pleased me to be able to be away from him, it gave me a kind of subtle thrill.

But it didn’t last long. We sort of gravitated back together and that summer we went to Paris. I got strep throat. Harrow met a stunning Jewess with long black hair, just like the girls we used to see in the Village. I had a fever, I was almost delirious and sometime near morning I heard them whispering in the bed next to me.

That fall we went to university. I remember him sneaking out of the apartment one night to play in a coffee house in Yorkville. He didn’t want anyone there in case he did badly or he chickened out or whatever. Later that night, I heard him climb up the stairs. I was in the living room. He sat down on the couch, his guitar case beside him. He was pale, excited. “I was all right," he said. He nodded. "Yes, I was. I may have played too long, I'm not sure, but they said I was good, I heard someone say it in the crowd, in the middle of a quiet part of the song, they said, he's really good. But I may have played too long, I don't know, one song too many."

He looked away puzzled.

I felt like putting my arms around him, like protecting him from anything that might ever hurt him.

In those days I had a girl friend named Zinta Strom, she was a polack, a cute little thing, very bright, with a kind of pushed-in face. I liked her but things weren't very sexy between us, I don't know why, they just weren't.

Anyway. Late one afternoon, Harrow and I lay like crashed fighters on the carpet. We were stoned on sleeping pills.

"I've got a real boner for Zinta," he said. "A real one."

I nodded dreamily and after a moment I scribbled her phone number in a child's scrawl and handed it to him. *I gave poor Zinta away!*

Later, satisfied, but a little sleepy, I drifted off to my room and passed out. I think I heard Zinta on the stairs just as I went under.

I woke up a couple of hours later and lay there in a sort of stupor, trying to collect my wits, when suddenly I remembered what I'd done. I bolted out of bed and dashed to the foot of the stairs.

"Zinta, Zinta," I called meekly.

I arrived just in the nick of time. Zinta, a little stunned by the turn of events, turned out to have her own thoughts about the new arrangement.

She came back down the stairs, I fell into her arms, I took her into my room, I wept bitter tears of love, I may even have porked her. I was that relieved. I mean the idea of Harrow banging her, of her doing all the things to him that she did to me, well it just made me spin with terror. For a couple of hours there I thought I was in love. I really did.

But sure, I know, it had nothing to do with Zinta; it was boys being homos.

Zinta and I drifted apart over summer vacation, I got another girlfriend, a chain-smoking asthmatic, and sometime that fall Zinta took up with Harrow, and that was fine. They were a good pair actually: he used to get her to whip him.

I know how that sounds. *Tie him up? Whip him?* Harrow was into that stuff. He liked to get his ass whipped. And you'd be surprised how many girls, fresh-faced creatures from private schools, got into it with him. The funny thing is, when Harrow talked about it, it never seemed sordid; he made it funny, it sounded like a freshly tossed salad.

But one night, a few years later, when Harrow was at law school, he fucked someone, I don't know who, presumably a girl, but Zinta found out. Maybe he took a couple of them snoozy pills and told her. They were always making you do stupid things. Anyway, a couple of nights later I dropped by the Flying Food Circus for a drink. And guess who was were? Zinta. She was sitting at the bar, cool as a cucumber, smoking a cigarette. I drank two bottles of white wine and went back to her place and dry humped her on the couch.

I didn't see Harrow again for five years.

Sometimes I think I did it to pay him back for Jamaica, for taking that other boy. Other times I think it's because I'm just plum mean. I don't honestly know.

I heard things about him. I heard he was still with Zinta Strom. Sort of. I heard he bought a house in Callington, a small, affluent farming community thirty miles north of the city. I heard his father died in a helicopter crash, I heard he drank too much, had "behaved badly" at a wedding; lured a bridesmaid into a cupboard and asked her to show him her tits. I had to laugh. Who did they think they were inviting? Harrow was the kind of guy who could get up in the middle of a formal dinner party and take a bath upstairs; and after about twenty minutes, most of the guests would be up there with him, sitting around the side of the tub, keeping him company.

I didn't see what the big deal was, but I confess: The fact that Harrow appeared to have lost the capacity to be eternally forgiven intrigued me, made me feel slightly better about having had him drop like a stone from my life.

I saw him once. It was a drizzly February day, he was making a left-hand turn in his car and he pretended not to see me. Then another time: I was at a party out in the Beaches and walked into the living room. A man with wild, frizzy hair bent over a guitar. He had his ear bent down to the box, he was trying to hear himself play. I stepped back as if I'd walked into a pane of glass. I retreated back into the kitchen and sat with the sweating cheeses and the lemons until I got up my nerve to stick my nose back in the party. He was gone. He must have heard I was there. A guy I didn't like stopped me. "Wasn't that Harrow Winncup?" he said. "Didn't you two guys used to be pals?"

He had a nose for trouble between people, this guy, he was the sort of fellow who turned up at your girlfriend's the night after a bad fight.

Some nights, when fog settled on the streets, when the air tinkled with an inexplicable excitement, I missed Harrow keenly. I walked through the university campus, hoping to run into him. I never did. Sometimes I found myself talking to him out loud, replaying a story. But I didn't look him up. I think I was afraid he'd say something so cruel to me, something so confidential and informed, that it'd knock me to the ground.

The truth is, during those five years, I wasn't that preoccupied with Harrow. There were other things to think about. I met a long-limbed, long-fingered actress in a bar. Her name was Kalie Buckelle and she was smashed. She smoked rugged cigarettes, leaning forward, both elbows on the table and gazed at me with undisguised interest. God, I thought, there's not a sordid bone in her body.

There's a long blank after that; I remember looking out a window on a farm in the prairies; I remember seeing a pregnant Kalie walking across a green field with her mother, a tiny tractor puttering soundlessly across the horizon behind them.

I remember turning on the radio in my study once; it was in the middle of the night and I heard a small stirring behind me. I had quite forgotten the baby was there.

We took a holiday. Kalie sold a bond to buy her ticket. We left the baby with her mother and went off to Jamaica together; but after four days, she came back from the ocean one day, her face red, and said, "That's enough of the Caribbean. I miss my bunny." So a couple of days later she flew home; I stayed on.

"Don't be unfaithful to me," she said. I took a bus to the far end of the island, to Port Antonio, a dull, pretty little fishing town where there's nothing to do except drink gin in a second-floor joint called the Roof. It didn't open till midnight; young black schoolgirls from the outlying towns arrived by bus; God knows how they got up in the morning. Reggae music thumped, the bass notes so penetrating that they seemed to interfere with the rhythm of your heart. By three in the morning the place steamed like a swamp. I stayed there till dawn and then walked home just as the fishing boats set off into the blue, blue water. In the afternoons, I awoke hung over, had breakfast somewhere, then came back to the hotel. I opened the windows, the ocean air blew the curtains apart, I read *Under the Volcano* aloud and I waited to go to the Roof.

One night, near three in the morning, a round-faced blond girl from the University of Indiana struck up a conversation with me at the bar. She was taking a course in urban planning in Kingston. Odd place to do that but nevertheless. She had that effortless gregariousness of a young American college student. You could almost smell the assumptions of privilege.

"I like you," she said. She had to lean over and shout in my ear. I could smell her body, her perspiration.

Fifteen hundred miles north, the wall clock clicked in the dark kitchen and Kalie Buckelle fidgeted in her sleep.

Once you open the door on that stuff, it's almost impossible to get it shut again.

The rest followed, not swiftly, but inevitably, and a little while later Kalie left me. She and the little boy, Jesse, moved across the bridge to the Greek side of town. It took a long time for it to hit me, that she was gone, and until it did, it was not a bad time, to be honest. I spent a year in a bar, it was a cheerful place, like a club for divorced fathers. There were advertising men, high-school teachers, a stockbroker, off-duty waitresses, a private detective, a traveller. . . . They all knew each other and at five o'clock on a Friday afternoon they came from all over the city. They filed through the door of the Circus with the high spirits of children after a final exam. They took off their coats, they stepped up to the bar, they waited to catch the bartender's eye. Sometimes I wonder if any of us has been as happy since then as we were that very moment at the bar, ordering the first drink on a Friday night.

Sometimes the door opened and a man with wild hair stepped into the bar. I'd see him in the mirror and I'd think God, that's him! What a perfect time to turn up. But when I turned around it was always someone else.

But after a while, after a year of it, I figured I owed myself something better. So I wrote a novel. I spent the whole summer writing it. That seemed like a long time then, a real commitment. I can't recall the plot, it was about a jazz musician I think, but on the first day of May I picked it up from the typist's and took myself out to lunch at a French restaurant. I had a good expensive meal–brochette d'agneau with tiny carrots –and then I ordered a coffee and opened up the book and began to read. I read ten pages, it was pretty good, then another ten pages. I was so excited I had to stand up and pace back and forth beside my table; and then the book fell apart like an overcooked chicken. Three hundred pages later I felt sick with disappointment and appalled at the amount of money I'd spent. I put the book in my sack and paid the bill and wandered off miserably down the sidewalk. Sometime that afternoon I decided to give up writing forever.

I enrolled in teacher's college. But, funny thing, I quite liked teaching, I liked the give and take, I liked the smell of schools, I liked the sound of lockers slamming. I didn't have a full-time post, I travelled around town, replacing sick teachers here and there. I never applied for a full-time position, I was afraid I'd get one. There's a saying that what a man does for a living is usually what he does best and that scared the pants off me, the idea of just being a teacher. Which I was of course, not even a real teacher, but I pretended it was something else, an adventure, a preparation.

But I liked it, I have to admit, it galvanized me. I burst out of the school doors on a Friday afternoon and I felt great, busy and tired, and by the time I got to the bar I realized, just fleetingly, that the best time of the week and the day was already behind me.

And that bit about not writing anymore–there was nothing tragic about it, not really. I dreamt I had a big talent and I didn't. But I did have some, I knew that, and after a while I drifted back into writing–on the side, of course. Small jobs. I even made a few bucks writing brochures for dental health; three booklets: I still remember the titles–*Dental Dilemmas, Stop Gum Disease,* and my favourite, *Power Eating*. And that led to other jobs: bank brochures, financial reports, ad copy for an aerobics studio, a film festival program. I even got a grant to write a play; it didn't work out but that wasn't a tragedy either: the point is, between teaching and *Power Eating,* I was doing fine.

There were dark moments when an ungifted friend published a book. I never resented the real thing, never begrudged real talent, ever, but a half-assed writer wanking in the newspaper as if he's Malcolm Lowry, it induced a kind of vertigo.

When an old girlfriend published a novel, I thought I had the flu for a couple of days. I rushed through it to see what she'd said about me. I liked the bit where she said I slept with my thesis adviser. It's not true but it's the sort of lie that flatters me. But what I didn't like, not at all, was the implication that *she* was the one to leave *me.* I almost phoned her up over that one.

Chapter Three

Then one night at the circus I got drunk and phoned Harrow. It was fall then too. Always the fall with Harrow, the season of new girlfriends, the smell of new notebooks, the real beginning of the year.

I had a stiff martini, the waitress gave me a wink, said she'd meet me after work, and, transported by a kind of invulnerable enthusiasm, I slipped down off my bar stool and went to the house phone and dialled his number from memory.

The phone rang three times, then a voice like a cold jewel answered. It was her. It was his mother. I asked for Harrow. There was a pause.

"Who is this?"

"It's Christian Blackwood."

There was another significant pause. Florence Winncup had learnt the use of silence. She let it go on until I was just about to speak, about to explain what didn't need explaining, when she cut in.

"How are you, Christian?"

"Fine," I said.

"Harrow's not here, Christian." Another pause. "Can I give him a message?"

"No," I said hesitantly.

"Why don't you leave a number? He can phone you back."

"Is he at the Callington house?"

It caught her off guard. I knew I'd hit it.

"I think he's out for the evening," she said.

I went back to the bar and had another martini. I ate the olive and downed it in one swallow. It wasn't cold enough. I knew there'd be trouble and I braced myself. I concentrated, just to get through it. I winced, then shuddered. I felt a slight nudge, like the tentative pull of a big fish on the line, then another, firmer pull; the bar light softened, something opened in the mirror in front of me, my features went soft and I soared up with the current. I got down from my stool again and went back to the house phone. I called information and got a listing for a Harrow M. Winncup in Callington. I dialled quickly, I could feel my heart thumping under my raincoat, I wished I'd had a third martini when suddenly the line went silent and a voice, a strange, tentative voice answered the phone.

"Hello," said the voice. It bore the tones of someone who wasn't sure if he should answer, or even be where the phone was ringing, but someone who, out of curiosity or obligation, has picked it up anyway. "Harrow," I said.

"Christian?" he said, as if intrigued by the idea, as if, even while he held the phone, he was warming to the notion.

"Christian ..." he repeated. In the background I could hear people, a small, noisy party, men and women. That was good. It meant, in all probability, that Harrow was loose and slammed and having a good time.

"I was just sitting here in the Circus and I thought to myself, I should give Harrow a call. I just should."

A pause.

"I know the Circus, don't I?"

"Yeah, we came in here about twelve years ago," I said.

"Twelve years ago," he said. "Jesus."

A car salesman, short and tubby, came into the Circus.

"People tell me all *sorts* of things about you . . . " I began.

Someone at his end shouted something. He put his hand over the phone. I heard him speak, but I couldn't make out what he said. He came back on.

"Quite a ruckus here," he said.

I put my hand over my ear, even though there was no noise.

"Do you want to get together sometime, Harrow? Have a drink or a beer or something?"

I could see his face clearly, a concerned, wrinkled brow. Harrow never kicked a man on the floor. I could feel him thinking. He was calculating something.

"Sure," he said.

A man laughed in the background.

"Do you know the Panama Club?" he asked.

The Panama Club was a stripper's bar at the foot of Yonge Street.

"I've got a studio over top," he said.

"No kidding?"

He couldn't resist a boast. "I'm in a band. We're not bad."

"What day should I come?" I asked.

"Tuesday?"

"Tuesday's perfect," I said.

That Tuesday, I gave myself lots of time to get to the Panama Club. It was a half hour walk from Chinatown. I must have been nervous because I had to stop at a student cafeteria to take a pee. I was talking to myself, playing out the conversation I imagined we'd have.

It was a fall day, bright as polished copper; it made me feel optimistic the way you do in that weather. I went down Yonge Street and crossed the streetcar tracks. It gets shitty below there, the people get ugly, bad skin, eyes too close together. It made me a tad impatient that Harrow was down there. He was always drawn to these neighbourhoods; he thought they were real, you know, exotic and literary. They gave me the creeps, made me want to have a fucking bath.

The street narrowed and funnelled me into the arcades and junk shops and cheap clothing stores and record shops and skin-book emporiums and strip houses and triple-movie joints. A junkie stood in the doorway of a donut shop, he looked like a ghost, skinny arms and fucked-up shoes; it's always the shoes. You can always tell how fucked up someone is by their shoes. I don't know why.

I stopped in front of the Panama Club. I went in. It was so dark inside I couldn't see anything. Tiny orange tadpoles swam over my pupils; I waited for my eyes to adjust. The place stank of stale cigarette smoke; it was in the carpets, it coated the mirrors, the table tops, the flesh of the girls who worked there. You could never get it out.

Table dancers moved between the tables. They were very pretty. It was a good joint.

Somewhere near the back of the room, a white hand waved at me. It only waved once and then fell out of sight. I picked my way gingerly through the gloom until I stood over top of him, looking down.

"Is that you?" I said.

I meant it as a joke but it hit a chord somewhere.

"I've put on a little weight," he said, half rising from his chair.

"That's not what I meant," I said quickly. "You look splendid." But it was hard to say for I could hardly make out his features. Except to say that he was a bigger man now, there was a bulk about him I didn't remember, a beefiness. He exuded a physical strength, even more than before, and its effect on me was to make me feel ungainly and oddly frivolous. It would take a lot to kill him, I thought.

But something was different, very different from the phone call. He was cold sober and tense. His lips were pressed tightly together. The Zinta business appeared to have pricked him with fresh anger. He was not alone. A man with a flat, predatory face sat beside him. He surveyed me unselfconsciously through two small black holes, like pistol barrels.

"This is Pascal," Harrow said. The man nodded. I extended my hand. For a second I thought he might not take it. He shifted his weight, removed a laconic hand from the pocket of a windbreaker and shook mine. He was very strong.

In spite of the heat and the close quarters, Harrow wore a winter scarf and an old sports coat. I took comfort in that, it was an old familiar island, something to throw a rope to.

"So how are you?" I said cheerfully. The man's unsmiling presence distracted me, made me feel transparently phony.

"Hung over," Harrow said and shovelled a forkful of Chinese food into his mouth. The fork was too small, it looked like a child's toy and he was eating from a tin-foil take-out container. Harrow never had great table manners, my mother pointed that out the first time he came to dinner. But there was something aggressive, something deliberately coarse, about the way he hunched his bulk over his food and shovelled it in with that silly white fork.

His friend regarded me impassively, an empty beer glass in front of him. There was something proprietorial about his manner with Harrow, like an animal protecting a kill.

"You should watch out for Chinese food," I said, searching Harrow's plate with my eyes.

He looked up; a glint of amusement cut through the hangover.

"What?" he said.

"They coat it with MSG. To keep it fresh. It makes your eyes roll back in your head."

He looked at me long and hard.

His companion rose from the table.

"Be right back, Jack," he said.

I looked at Harrow.

"Everyone calls me Jack down here," he said. "It's my stage name."

"Oh," I said, surprised. It worried me. People who change their names worry me. He finished the last forkful, wiped his fingers and sat back.

"Whew," he said. He was feeling sick; even in that dreadful light you could see his colour was off.

"Who was that?" I asked, gesturing toward the empty chair beside him.

"He used to be the best left-handed sax player in the city," Harrow said.

"Really?" I said.

His lips spread in a wide, mute smile and he nodded his head slowly up and down. He was plainly impressed. "I could tell you stories ..." he began, but at that moment Pascal emerged from the dark doorway. He sat down, lit an Export A and whispered something to Harrow with a small, familiar smile. Harrow wrinkled his brow. That was his guilt wrinkle. I remembered it from Forest Hill.

"Really?" he said.

Pascal nodded. He knew Harrow, knew that wrinkle always preceded a capitulation.

Harrow leaned across the table.

"I've got a meeting," he said. I must have looked blank. But then I understood. He was leaving. I let the friendliness fall from my face. This was too much, too rude. I raised my eyebrows and nodded my head.

"Stick around and see the band," he said. "They're pretty good."

I nodded again and they left. I sat at the table for only a moment longer; smoke hung over the bar in a red cloud. Later that night, my clothes still stank of it.

Florence Winncup was an interesting dangerous woman who built herself, as she did her children, from the outside. She grew up in Port Albion on the shore of Lake Huron. Her father died when she was little. She dropped out of high school, went to secretarial college, and got engaged to a boy who worked in the local hardware store. Then she met a much older man, a red-faced, hard-drinking lumber baron who hired her, seduced her (he thought), then married her. He even gave her former boyfriend a job, made him a foreman in his planing mill. "Don't ever apologize for who makes your dick hard, son, never!" This was Harrow's father.

When Harrow and his younger sister were still children, his father fell out of the sky one day in a helicopter. Pilot error. No one understood why. "I wasn't even half cut," the old man hollered when they pulled him from the wreckage. "I want someone with a pair between his legs to tell me what the fuck happened!" They sent him down to Toronto, took blood, took x-rays, CAT scans and then they found it. Multiple sclerosis. Gave him eighteen months to live.

By the time he got to Jamaica he couldn't hit a tennis ball. Missed it by a foot and a half. While Harrow and his sister played on the beach at Runaway Bay, Florence Winncup bullied her husband back on to the tennis court and threw balls at him. This went on for months, the old man out there, sweating, red faced, swinging "like a goddamn spastic monkey"–but she kept him at it, wouldn't let him fade into death. And then one day, just before sunset, she lobbed a ball over the net and he hit it. He saw it coming and he hit it.

"Well, I'll be a son of a bitch," he explained and went inside for a bourbon.

A couple of days later, he hit another one.

"I might as well build a house," he said. "This looks like it might take a while."

I assume he meant dying.

He went into town, hired a dozen men, and they built a beautiful pink house at the end of the beach. "If you want to do something for a nigger," he explained to Harrow, "don't feel sorry for him. Give him a job!"

On his birthday, two years after he arrived, he disappeared for a couple of hours after dinner, in the vicinity of a vacationing nurse from Colorado Springs. It was time to go home.

A few weeks later, a boy with a brown sack on his shoulder stopped his bicycle in front of my house.

Chapter Four

A month passed. The leaves had fallen from the trees, a cold wind blew up from the lake, men in pea jackets shook hands on street corners and walked briskly away.

I went into the Flying Food Circus for a drink. It was a Friday night, the place was filling up. I drank there for I don't know how long; it got dark, no one went home for dinner, the glasses lay glittering on the bar, full of gold and silver and froth. The waitresses glided among the shadows and then someone I didn't know came in, he left the door open and the wind blew in. It was a cold fall wind, it smelt of diamonds, it swirled in the bar, it sent my thoughts dancing and then before I knew it I was out on the street. It was Hallowe'en; there were skeletons and hobgoblins and men dressed as beautiful women and university boys hanging from the window of a white limousine; there were girls in turtlenecks, there was a splatter of blood like coins on the sidewalk, there was a man staring up the side of a building, there was a shoe in the gutter. I pushed down Yonge Street, it teemed, it shimmered with excitement, with other nights when Harrow and I had steamed down the street, eager to fall in love, to be writers, to study philosophy, to go to Paris, to see the Beatles, to bicycle through Scotland ... only Harrow, it seemed, could understand a night like tonight.

What made me go back there that night, I don't know. Lonely, maybe. No other friends. No girlfriend; all of them, I guess. You can't replace old friends like Harrow. It's like a tooth falling out. Nothing comes in to replace it. New people take effort, you've got to start all over again and I couldn't be bothered.

A little while later, I was standing outside the Panama Club. There was a glass door on the side, I went in and up a long flight of stairs. There was a metal door at the top, wrinkled and rusted. I knocked on it. There was no answer. I knocked again and then I noticed a note, taped to the middle of the door. It was in Harrow's distinctive handwriting, big and round, and it said *Downstairs.* So I went back down the stairs and into the bar. Harrow and his band were humping and grooving through an old cover.

Boom, boom, boom, boom,
Gonna shoot you right down
Boom, boom, boom, boom,
Right offa' your feet.

It surprised me but there was something sort of grubbily magnificent about Harrow up there: jowly, rough looking, twenty pounds overweight. I remembered suddenly a conversation we'd had just before he went to law school. I'd noodled my finger at him. I said, well man, you can kiss the music goodbye. He said, no, that was bullshit. "I'll get a degree and I won't practise."

"That's what every asshole on Bay Street said when *they* went to law school," I complained. "And now they're sniffing each other's assholes and talking dirty at lunch."

Well, he wouldn't have any of it, I remember, and by God, he was right. It wasn't a great band, it wasn't a great spot to be playing, there was no big recording contract looming around the corner, not for this band, but he was up there, he was doing it. He'd delivered.

In the dark and dirty light, Harrow and the band were moving through "High Heel Sneakers." There were five of them, a black drummer, a keyboardist, a hot-shot white kid with a white Telecaster (he watched himself play in the mirror), Harrow and Pascal on tenor saxophone.

"*Better bring along some boxin' gloves,*" Harrow sang, "*In case some fool might want to fight.*"

Then he stepped away from the microphone and let the kid go. He was a real little wizard, this narrow-hipped boy; he could play like the blazes.

A red spotlight came up from the floor. At the next table a short-haired girl in white overalls put her feet in her boyfriend's lap, lit a cigarette, and talked about how shitty the band the night before had been. She had white, creamy skin, like a baby. From the kitchen floated the smell of greasy hamburgers, french fries. A pretty waitress in her forties moved among the tables. An old man in a toque with a white beard shuffled across the room. Two lank-haired men sat at the lip of the stage. A curly-haired weight-lifter came in, hands in his pockets, and stood in the doorway. A pair of bearded, thin men sat near the back. They liked working-class bars.

Harrow stepped back to the mike. The band kept rolling.

"Welcome," he said. "I'm Mr. Jack Ash." The drummer whacked a rim shot. "And these things behind me are the Shotgun Express." The band hushed down, kept playing, like a whisper. A microphone shrieked. Harrow pushed it away from a speaker. The shriek stopped.

"We've come to play the blues. If you like the blues, stick around; if you don't, stick around anyway till the place fills up."

Someone guffawed.

"Eat, drink and be merry," he said. "If Mary doesn't show, pick the next best."

The band picked up tempo, swung into "Let the Good Times Roll."

"In case you don't know, this is the Panama Club and cat exchange. The only pussy you'll get here has four legs and will eat you out of house and home."

The band kicked up an octave. "The other kind has two legs and will do the same damn thing."

He waited a beat.

"And you can't get *that* at the Humane Society."

The baby-faced girl laughed. "I love these guys," she said.

The band swung into "Black Cat Blues."

An Indian woman slumped forward on the table and slept.

"I believe that cat is feelin' the heat," went the song. *"I got tomcats all around my place."*

He sounded good. The band chugged forward.

"I bet when my black cat comes home tonight, she'll have a smile all over her face."

At the back of the bar, the Oriental owner sat expressionless by the cash register. The Indian woman, enormously fat, got up, her eyes almost crossed, and staggered toward the bathroom. I ducked her glance.

The band picked up the pace, jumped into shuffle time. A chair fell over. Someone lit a cigarette.

"Feel free to dance," Harrow said.

No one did. The square patch of dusty cement in front of the stage remained empty.

"Bring it down, boys," he said,"bring it down." He went down to a high-hat cymbal, a bass guitar, the occasional explosive rim shot.

"I'm sending this song out," he said, "to those who have been wronged in love." Beat. "I don't know anyone who's ever been righted in love, do you?" Rim shot.

Then he counted the band in: one, two, three, four, five, and they swung into a medium-tempo twelve-bar. The Indian woman emerged from the bathroom. With great concentration she made it back to her table. I found myself drifting off, the heat, the cigarette smoke. I found myself watching Pascal. I tried to imagine him as a child. It must have been because I had spent the day with Jesse; I had bathed him, soaped his fat arms and legs, dried his hair, wrapped him in a towel and sent him marching like a little prince out of the steamy bathroom. I had gazed at his excited face, his limbs, with such love that it scared me, made me look away. I tried to imagine Jesse up there on that stage, playing the saxophone, all grown up. It seemed like an inconceivable thought that he'd ever grow so large and then suddenly I felt that flutter of panic, that he was so unprotected in the world, that his body, his bones and chest and skin were all so fragile, so easily pierced. I stopped myself. But when I looked at Pascal, or Harrow, or the guitar kid or the drunken Indian woman, I saw them all as children in grown-up bodies and the notion, just the sheer idea of it, softened the world for me; and I softened with it.

Then it was time to "pause for a cause." Harrow said they'd be right back, reminded us the band accepted free drinks, and they closed down the tune. The music stopped, the moment lost its stature, the tableau deflated into a group of sloppily dressed men talking on a stage. The spotlight went off. The men stepped down off the stage and headed to the back of the bar. Only Harrow remained. He looked down at the red body of his guitar and, as if preoccupied with an unrelated thought, ran a pick over the strings. A rich chord ran through the sound system, so pristine you could hear the plink of the plastic pick on the steel strings. No one noticed; people talked, smoked, ordered drinks. The band settled at a table. Cigarette packs were thrown down. The drummer went to the pay phone. The body of Harrow's guitar caught the light for a second and gleamed like a fish in the sunlight.

Then very simply, privately, he began. He was looking at the floor, at a sheet of legal paper held in place with his foot, containing the lyrics to a song he must have written only that day. It was called "Portrait of a Lady." It was a sad, slow ballad about a lost school girl. The fact that Harrow never raised his head gave the moment an extraordinary intimacy, and as I watched him up there, hunched over under a soft yellow light, a stocky man no longer young, no longer handsome, completely absorbed in the song, not performing, for no one was watching, but simply feeling his way through it for the first time, this lovely, heartbroken ballad, I had a moment of intense, private revelation. Harrow Winncup was, for those few seconds, everything I had always suspected him of being, as grand, as gifted, as unique; and my affection for him, my enormous expectations for his life, were thoroughly and absolutely vindicated.

As the voice faded, the girl in white overalls said simply, "Wow."

I lingered at the edge of the spotlight while Harrow left the stage and sat down. I waited until he looked casually around the bar, until he saw me, and then I raised my arm, very simply. It was a friendly, easy wave, it didn't matter now, we were square, I knew that, I just wanted him to know I wasn't ducking out or sneaking around any more. I raised my hand, I gave him a short, warm smile, and then I stepped outside on to the street. And for the first time in a long time, in five years perhaps, maybe longer, I felt free of something.

I got twenty paces up the street, I was already thinking about something else, about how fast the time was going by, when I heard a voice call me from the doorway.

"Hey you, mister blister!"

Harrow stood in the doorway, holding on to the doorframe and leaning out into the street.

He shook his head, partly bemused, partly saddened.

"I missed you," he said. "I really did."

We went up to the studio after the last set, the band and a dozen people who'd come to see them play. It was a long, low-ceilinged room; a kick-boxing bag hung from the ceiling. Musical instruments lay about, a tan acoustic guitar, a mismatched set of drums, a music stand. There was a bunk bed, a beanbag chair, a dart board, an old-fashioned reel-to-reel tape recorder. Overhead lighting very bright. No windows, the back door swung open on to an alley. In the corner stood a card table littered with bottles of tequila and rum and gin, orange juice, Cokes, sliced lemons. This was a hard-liquor crowd; there wasn't a beer in sight, only a frightening bottle of Bull's Blood. I poured myself a screwdriver, a double, reached into a garbage bucket and pulled out a handful of ice and dumped it in my glass. I drank it in two gulps and poured another one.

It was a curious collection of people. One guy had a club hand, it was like a tortured lump of flesh, he kept it in his pocket; a girl had a walleye.... There's nothing wrong with a walleye, in fact it made her quite sexy. It's just that there seemed to be something wrong with everyone up there. Oh yes. My cousin Warren was there too. He was a disappointing young man, sweet-natured but weak and a fuck-up. He showed up later. Blind pissed, his features dripping down his skull like melted wax. He smelt too, he hadn't changed his shirt. At one point he came over and, putting his face real close to mine, kind of bent his head to the side and hollered into my ear: "Are you having a good time?"

But I liked Harrow, I liked being around him; he was a big, cheerful, noisy presence; he put out like mad for everyone and I liked that about him. Pascal was there too. I was aware of him all the time, of where he was in the room. He wore a blue T-shirt. He had arms like a fucking orangutan. The only way to stop a prick like that is with a gun.

There was a black guy there, Clayton, he was the drummer with the band; a good-looking son of a bitch, like a movie star, he wore an Ethiopian hat and a sleek leather jacket. But he couldn't hold his liquor and after a couple of belts of vodka he started coming at you. Just talking, implying stuff. I moved away from him. He caught up to me. "You got a problem talking to a black man?" he said. I ignored him, I wanted to keep my head down, keep a low profile. I was just glad to be there. But Clayton kept at it.

"Are you a rich boy or something?" he said and kind of left his jaw hanging open. "That why you don't like black folk?"

I moved away again, I stood in another part of the room. I started talking to a high-school principal; he seemed all right, at first anyway, then he told me, apropos of nothing, that his wife would never leave him, that he was smarter than she was. He pointed her out. She was a racy-looking little babe, an olive-skinned Sicilian, dark eyes, dark circles under them. I took a sort of surprised look at him. Talk like that was bad luck, like saying you're never going to get hit by a car or get cancer. It was asking for trouble. She was talking to my cousin, a drink in one hand, she was smoking a cigarette, blowing the smoke away from him. There was something accessible about her, getable, she was not taken care of, all the men she talked to sensed it, even if they pretended they were interested in what she was saying.

A pretty young woman with a tangle of fair hair crossed the room and whispered something in Harrow's ear. Standing beside him like that, I suddenly recognized her. It was Dorian Winncup, Harrow's kid sister. I hadn't seen her since she was fifteen. She was thin, tentative as a candle flame, with small, slightly discoloured teeth. Her skin was pale, her hair, like her brother's, was wild blond, and fell in frizzy waves to her shoulders. It accentuated the finesse of her features, a small nose, a nervous mouth, large, apprehensive eyes. But those eyes, they were slightly hooded now; she looked slammed. And there was, in her complexion, the softness of her skin, the feel, the texture that young skin takes when its owner wakes up, often, hung over.

I lost sight of her for a while. Then, while I was watching Harrow whip a long-bladed knife against the wall–it was some kind of contest they were having–I felt someone touch my arm. It was Dorian.

“Christian,” she said. “Is that you? I’m so … surprised.”

She touched my elbow again, very softly. “I’m working in my mother’s store,” she said. “She has a furniture store on Chester Square. Antiques. I bet I know what you think of that.” She raised her eyebrows ironically.

Warren collapsed on a green chesterfield and closed his eyes, a self-conscious smile of pleasure on his lips.

“You know,” Dorian said, standing close to me, “I used to like you an awful lot.”

She was wearing perfume. “Mother didn’t like you, did she?”

“No, she didn’t.”

I looked at her. I had a wild dangerous notion to kiss her. That she wanted me to.

“You’ve turned out very pretty,” I said.

She looked straight ahead. I wondered if she’d heard me. But a small, ironical smile of pleasure curled her lips. She knew I was looking at her.

“I painted that sign,” she said suddenly. Over the door was a garish, hand painted sign–*The Panama Club.* I saw Harrow watching me across the room.

“Oh,” I said. “Very nice.” She opened her mouth to say something else but stopped. Harrow came over.

“I want to show you something,” he whispered in my ear.

He led me to a back room, just off the bathroom, opened a padlocked door and took me into a small square box of a room. Inside there was a bed covered in a green blanket, a desk, a reading lamp, a book on the night table, *The Little Prince.* I sat down on the corner of the bed while he flushed out a mess of keys from his pocket and opened the cupboard. He swung the door open. Inside, there was a weapons collection: rifles, a machete, a spear, a pair of wooden nunchucks hung on the door peg, a grappling hook and rope, a throwing star. . . .

“Well,” I said. I felt him scrutinizing my face. “This is all new.” He reached in and pulled down an M16 assault rifle. He snapped open the bridge and handed it to me. I looked down the barrel, I could smell oil in the breech. I laid it on the bed.

"Can I?" I said. I was worried about staining the blanket.

"Sure," he said, "it's had worse than that on it."

He pulled down a gleaming black pistol.

"A nine-millimetre," he said. "That'll knock you across the room."

He laid it on the bed.

"You preparing for a take-over?" I said.

"Communists," he answered dead pan. "Everyone knows that when they come, it'll be across the Bering Strait on snow-mobiles."

"And what's this?" I said.

"Grappling hooks."

"And this?"

"A death star."

"Of course, a death star." I paused and frowned. "Do you have any machine guns?"

"It's just like you to ask for the only thing I don't have."

"How about a box of hand grenades? Now I really need one of those."

And then we sat down on the bed and talked with great pleasure about unimportant things.

Somewhere later in the evening, everyone pissed, Harrow and the keyboardist put on the boxing gloves. It was no big deal, no one paid any attention; they went into the centre of the room and smacked away at each other for a while.

The walleyed girl watched with self-conscious seriousness, as if she was the only person in the room to understand the significance of what was going on, its subtext. Harrow always had a dope like that around, someone who didn't turn away when he puked. I wondered where Zinta Strom was, that loose-lipped tattletale. Someday when I was back in tight with Harrow I'd give that little cunt a talking to. But she wasn't there; she was still on the side, I imagined, like an extra order of toast. That was how Harrow liked to keep her. All those years Strom stayed in the wings, waiting to get invited into the Winncup family; poor dumb fuck, she hadn't figured out that Harrow's mother called the shots, that she'd never, ever, sit still for letting a polack into the family. But Zinta didn't know that. She had a fucking master's degree in French literature but she hadn't figured that out. Just what the fuck was she doing all those years in school? Honey, get your finger out of your snapper and wake up. No, Zinta was probably out in Mississauga right now, waiting for Harrow to call her, knitting a sweater for Mrs. Winncup, doing everything, waiting for the call that would never come. Meanwhile Harrow was porking the shorts off Wally. Wally the walleye. But like I said, even with her fucked-up eye, she was a sexy thing; a chick like that'd suck you dry if you gave her half a chance.

But she didn't get a chance because Harrow and his pal were whacking the shit out of each other in the middle of the room. That kind of masculine faggot foreplay makes me nervous; it's supposed to be fun but it's not, it can get ugly fast. There's too much underlying it, too much vanity at stake, and when the keyboardist gave Harrow a wallop on the side of the head I just laughed out loud. It was nerves but the room went silent and Harrow shot me a look and it wasn't good.

Clayton caught my eye; he made a cutting sign across his throat and pointed at me. I looked away but he was starting to piss me off. I used to be a pretty good boxer or at least I think I was and I started to entertain some pretty hostile ideas. Honestly, if that guy kept at me, maybe I'd give him a whirl myself. I mean out in the street he could whup me something awful; but in the ring, there are rules, like you can't kick or pull a gun, and for a fuckweed like Clayton, that may have been just too great a handicap.

Harrow must have got pissed off because he came at the black guy windmilling, technique forgotten. The black guy knew he was in a bit of trouble; he tied him up tight, held him, whispered something in his ear, Harrow pulled his head away as if he didn't want to hear. They had their bodies pressed together, their sweat rubbed off on each other, it was extraordinarily intimate. And the black guy just held on to him, hugged him, and after a while Harrow just stopped struggling.

Clayton came over to me. "You're going to get your ass kicked, white boy. Laughing like that. You're going to get your ass whipped."

"Just a second," I said.

I went over to Harrow.

I was drunk now; it came easily and certainly.

"Do you think I can take that guy?" I said.

Harrow looked at him; he seemed to be appraising something.

"You might," he said. "You just might."

I went back to Clayton. "I'm going to knock that fucking hat right off your head," I said. "And I'm not going to do it because you're black. I'm going to do it because you're an asshole and you've been pissing me off all night."

So I put on the gloves, someone laced them up for me, and took off my glasses. But when I stood up, and the crowd cleared, I wasn't looking at Clayton. He was gone; there was no sign of him. I was looking at Harrow. He watched me impassively, coldly, and he was wearing boxing gloves.

Somebody gave me a little push from behind. Suddenly I was cold sober. Harrow came at me with his glove cocked back like a piston. It was clear he wanted to kick the shit out of me and he didn't care if he got hit a couple of times in the process. That's a bad man to be in a fight with. But if we were ever going to get past this Zinta Strom stuff I'd have to give him something. So I let him chase me for a while. I back-pedalled, the place went quiet, they knew something was up. Then I gave him his punch. I dropped my guard and in it came; but at the last second I lost my nerve, I threw up my gloves, the blow clanged off my forearm and deflected up on to my skull. I sort of staggered backwards like a bad actor in a western, but the force of the punch had been broken; we both knew that. I collapsed on the couch. I think I landed on someone. I don't know. There was a scream. I lay back, I pulled at the strings on my gloves with my teeth. Harrow loomed over me.

"Fuck," he said, quite forgetting himself. "I never got the knock-out punch in. Fuck, fuck, fuck." Then he spun around like a spoilt kid and stormed off across the room.

I took off the gloves. I dropped them on the floor. I wasn't quite sure what to do next. Then Dorian came over.

"Well, Mr. Christian," she said, "it's been lovely to see you again. I must be off."

"Hang on," I said.

Dorian and I started up Yonge Street. Hallowe'en was over. The children were home in bed. Only a single transvestite, wobbling on high heels, hurried down the street. I looked for the splash of blood but I must have missed it. We cut down a narrow sidestreet. Expensive stores lay side by side like jewels on a gold bracelet. Dorian stopped in front of a richly lit window. A brown armoire lay under a spotlight. Its brass knobs gleamed.

"That's our store," she said. "My mother's store."

We stood in front of the window looking in.

"There's just the two of you?" I said.

"Yep."

"You go in every day?"

"I try to. Sometimes I don't."

"What happens then?"

"We stay closed."

There was a dry self-irony to her that wasn't there as a child; it had evolved, I guessed, from her curious formality. Another way of keeping the world at bay. Believe the worst about yourself, say it first, before anyone else can.

"You should get a good look," she said. "We're thinking of burning it down."

I looked at her. A small butterfly smile teased her mouth.

"For the insurance. Know anyone who's interested?"

A cab drove by. Pascal's white, expressionless face stared out. We crossed a dark parking lot and had to step sideways to slide between two closely parked cars. My hand brushed her stomach.

We came out on University Avenue. It stretched long and lonely. A milk truck barrelled by.

"Isn't there another street we could take?" she said. "I never liked this street. It's too wide. It depresses me."

We walked on a block, then cut up through Chinatown. "Listen," I said, "who was that appalling asshole, the guy in the beret?"

"Pascal," she said. "He killed a guy."

"Bullshit."

"No really. Harrow loves him. He loves that stuff. He's got a taste for exotica. Like rare birds or turtles. . . . "

"How do you mean he killed a guy?"

"He killed a guy and he got off. Self-defense."

"When was this?"

"I don't know, years ago," she said wearily. "He put a rifle on a tripod, and shot a guy's heart out of his chest when he came up the stairs."

"Come on."

"He's a very, very bad man," she said. "I can't figure out what Harrow is thinking of."

We walked on in silence. It didn't make sense. I had a feeling it was bullshit, all of it, that Pascal had spun them a yarn and they'd fallen for it like a couple of real city slickers.

"Anyway," she said, "enough."

She looked up the street after a retreating milk truck.

"Can you imagine having a job like that?" she said.

"Like what?"

"Like driving that milk truck. Getting up at four o'clock in the morning. Day after day."

"I suppose you get used to it."

"No, you don't," she said. "Sometimes I look in a window or a house and say to myself, God, I'd just die if I were that person."

"Why?"

"Well, because they're not coming with me; they're getting left behind."

"Maybe they're leaving you behind."

"Well, they have to think that, don't they?"

The thought hung in the air, then popped.

"Oh," she said, surprised. "I've been tricked. Got anything to drink at your house?"

"No," I said. "I don't."

"Know any after-hours bars?"

I hesitated and she jumped in.

"Never mind. I'm tired. I'm just trying to find some way to make myself feel better. I should just go to bed. That's what I need."

"I could probably rustle up some rye or something."

But she'd decided.

"No, I'm being greedy."

We passed a delicious-smelling bakery.

"I had a boyfriend once who worked in a bakery. A lovely-smelling man. But I had such terrible allergies. I think my allergies drove him away. He lived in a ragweed field. I cried all the time. Nothing would stop it. Except a frost. I get shots now."

We cut through a park. On a bench, a couple was necking up a storm. The girl faced the man, her legs wrapped around his waist, her face buried in his hands. They were writhing and twitching and for a second I thought he might be inside her.

"My goodness," I whispered. It was meant to be funny but it sounded childish. Dorian said nothing, didn't even notice, and for a second she seemed like the older of the two of us. We passed under a leafy tree, then came out under a spotlight. I watched our shadows race over the grass and pass us. We moved up Starling Avenue, a quiet street of big lawns and big houses. We were near her house. I got ready to say goodbye.

"Do you want to see where I live?"

"Yes."

"Just come up and have a look around?"

"Yes."

We climbed a steep set of cement stairs. In the shadows by the door there was an intimate silence while she looked for her keys and I stood next to her, quite close. I was trying to smell her but the trees and the vegetation were too strong and I couldn't.

Then she withdrew a young hand from her pocket and inserted a single brass key in the lock and turned it. Light spilled out from a carpeted, silent hallway. A black, severe table stood in the foyer. A brass pot of potpourri sat on the table. "It smells like money in here," I said. A pile of letters lay on the floor. I picked them up. None for her. I flipped through them quickly. She didn't rush me. She just watched me read the names on the envelopes. It was very sexy the way she just stood there and watched. We climbed a set of carpeted stairs, our footsteps absorbed in the rugs. She unlocked another door and led me in a softly lit living room. Jazz peeped from a radio. A girl read a magazine on the sofa. She appeared to have been waiting. She had a round, brown body and a round face; she was doing math sums in a notebook on her lap. On the table beside her burned a green banker's lamp. From the doorway I could see into the bedroom. There was only one bed, a double, pink-topped, like a cake, with fluffy white pillows.

Dorian introduced me. The girl nodded politely at me, then returned to her sums. Neither she nor Dorian said anything else to each other. They both seemed tense. I had the feeling a quarrel was brewing, that it would erupt the moment I left. I also had the unpleasant feeling that I was being used, as either a shield or a provocation. I stayed only a few moments, offered a few banal observations about high school-students which interested no one, not even me. Dorian saw me to the foot of the stairs.

"Excuse my roommate," she said. "She's rather grumpy."

I gave her a peck on the cheek and, rather soberly, she bid me goodnight.

When she went back upstairs, I walked a half a block and then laughed out loud. It was a slightly forced, theatrical laugh.

I turned and headed home, put my feet up on the dining room table and poured myself a long, tall Scotch.

Chapter Five

But the next morning. Wow. I've been in hell before but nothing matches getting a supply-teaching call at 6:45 in the morning when you're hung over. It's like someone grabbing you by the neck and throwing you naked on to the floor. It felt like I was doing myself harm, just being up. Fifteen minutes later I was going through a set of motions I had grown to despise. Fill the kettle, brush my teeth, take a pee, take down my jacket, open it up, smell under the arms (don't let the kiddies get that on you), throw it on the bed, pull a shirt from the drawer, shake it out, put it on, roll up the sleeves because they're too short. Put on grey flannels, not too fast or the ass will rip. Put on socks, take off kettle, make coffee, check the time on Kalie's green wall clock.

I ran over the events of the evening. Thank God I hadn't gone back later, talked about it, gotten sloppy about it. It might just have done the trick, that little two-step with the boxing gloves.

Outside, a dog-faced woman pushed a baby stroller to the corner. I put on my jacket, did up my fly, went to the front door, surveyed the apartment, went back into the bathroom, squeezed a deodorant can between two shirt buttons and gave myself a squirt; went to the door again, came back into the bathroom, blew my nose, checked for toothpaste on the sides of my mouth and then hurried up the street for the bus that took me to the subway which roared under that dark movie theatre.

That morning the subway was full of monsters, glazed and brutal featured. It was a blindingly bright day–why were these creatures out?–and the train shot uptown, through a vast graveyard. Down one bank where the sun hadn't reached yet, the stones, white and black marble, lay in cool green shade and I wanted to get off the train and go lie among them. Join the rest of my family. Get this violent, jarring nonsense over with. But we roared on, me hanging from a cord by my arm, trying not to breathe on anyone. By the time I got to school I was sucking on a Scotch mint. I hadn't eaten, but it made my stomach think I had, and those little digestive acids, they started squirting out, getting ready to burn down a piece of toast or a muffin but finding nothing there, they went to work anyway and started to eat into the floor of my stomach. Or that's how I saw things, booming up through the city.

I checked in at the front desk; I'd taught there before, it was a level-three school for slow learners. I got the assignment sheet and wandered down the hall, still sweaty, and went into a classroom at the far end. The bell rang; a ragged batch of girls, black, white, Chinese, a quartet of surly Jamaicans, filed in and sat down. I was taking attendance when a white girl in tight jeans stood up at the back of the class and started for the door.

"Charlene, where are you going?" I said with a touch of impatience.

She opened her small round mouth. "I've got to go to the bathroom, sir," she said and smirked at a friend.

I wasn't in the mood for this; I wasn't in the mood to be back in the classroom, I realize that now.

"Charlene," I said heavily, "you know better than to get up in my class and wander off. . . . " I sounded like Queen Victoria.

"I got to go to the bathroom, sir, I got come in my mouth."

I sent her to the Vice Principal but I didn't call down to see if she went. I didn't care. It was my fault really, I should have seen it coming. Not pushed her so hard. Besides, Charlene's father was a short brutal Portuguese; he'd just smack the shit out of her and tomorrow she'd be back sucking off someone else in a van in the school parking lot. I hoped she took the day off.

At recess I wandered the halls. It was very sexy. I loved the way the girls smelt. I couldn't stand the staff room. No one ever talked to me. It wasn't personal. I finally understood that. They didn't want to waste the steam, just like farmers talking slowly.

A kid in a turned-around baseball cap, an unlit cigarette in his hand, grinned at me.

"Ever been stoned, sir?"

I ignored him.

I ran into a teacher on the second floor. He was my age with black-rimmed glasses and a spotty brown suit. Dandruff flaked his shoulders. He couldn't stop looking at the girls, his hunger was almost tangible. "These kids," he said, "they get more ass than a toilet seat." He'd been talking dirty for so long he hadn't realized where he'd landed. It was private dirty twaddle. He kept talking. I stared out the window; he kept talking; I nodded my head. I thought he'd get the hint. He offered me a Valium. I said no thanks. He kept talking. I stood there staring out the window. It was so beautiful out there on that playing field; a wisp of paper, a candy-bar wrapper, blew across the grass. I followed it all the way to the road. It seemed as if I couldn't move. The sun roasted me through the glass, it felt delicious on my face. Down the hall, a slow organ march poured from the gym; it was a drama class, and I found myself thinking about my mother, I don't know why. The evening with Harrow had opened up something in me. I suddenly focused very clearly on her, she was wearing a grey wool dress with a silver belt, she was sitting opposite me in a living room in a house in Mexico, a big white room with a fire. She looked amused, engaged, she was just sitting forward to say something to me, to respond to me. It made me ache to think she was gone, it surprised me how much it hurt, almost made me swoon. God, to sit only for a moment, to sit down and talk to her, to catch up, to tell her everything ... I suddenly had the most overpowering sense of wanting to cry. The bell rang.

I went upstairs and babysat four sweet deaf kids in the special-education department while they did desk work. At least it was quiet up there. But the boredom was exhausting and by lunch I was starving. I went down to the student cafeteria and got a tray and ate two full lunches, mashed potatoes and gravy. I sat alone at a table. No one joined me. Finally a skinny-armed Trinidadian boy with a wonky glass eye came over and asked if he could sit down. I said sure. I didn't know which eye to address. He had an orange. I could smell it. He offered me a piece. I thanked him. I felt a wave of sleepiness coming on. I thought it best to take a walk, get a newspaper, keep moving before I fell asleep in my potatoes. I left the cafeteria. A fat boy came through the doors as I went out. He carried a giant black radio and he was looking for someone to listen to it with. In his other hand he had a bag of ketchup potato chips. He was saving those too. Some days those schools just broke your heart.

In the afternoon the police came and arrested the four Jamaican girls. They'd knocked off a clothing store during lunch, nothing violent, they'd just pushed their way into the store and grabbed armloads of jeans and run out; but they'd been greedy, they took more than they could carry and they left a trail of dropped items all the way back to the school. The cops took them away, angry and unrepentant. The whole scene depressed me.

I put the class on study and read my newspaper.

After school I saw Charlene in the parking lot. She had a cigarette curled in the palm of her hand and she was waiting for her friends. We pretended not to see each other.

Chapter Six

Over the next couple of weeks Harrow and I drifted back together. I don't know what we did that fall, not much really, drank, did pills, got wrecked and gooned around downtown, but it was a happy, happy time for me.

When I think back on my life now, on the life I had in those days, I wonder that I didn't despair. I admire my optimism. It seems, on the face of things, brave. I was a thirty-three-year-old alcoholic supply teacher jerking off in the boys' bathroom to fantasies of oral sex with fifteen-year-old students with names like Minky and Donna Lee. Yet I remained convinced I was about to inherit the life I deserved. I carried about inside me an inextinguishable ball of sunshine, I don't know where it came from.

Harrow came back at a good time though. I needed an ally, I needed a hit of the old magic, someone to whisper "Of course you will" on those black rainy fall mornings when the sound of wet tires seeped into my heart.

I have a clear image of that time: Harrow and I, upstairs over top of the Panama Club, huddled over a card table, weak with laughter, drinking vodka at eleven o'clock in the morning ... it seemed like the best possible time to be alive, the best possible place, as if there were nothing else conceivable to do, as if the whole world, streaming by down on the street, as if they were somehow missing the point, somehow to the side of the action.

Pascal got arrested; he tried to kill his stepfather with a ball-peen hammer so they kicked him out of the band. Well, they didn't really have to. He was in the slammer.

I did a little supply teaching. I wrote another brochure on dental hygiene. I wrote a couple of songs for the band; not the music, just the words.

Harrow moved into my flat for a while. I can't remember why. I think he had a row with someone. I didn't care. It was nice having him around; he gave things a sense of occasion, he just always did.

After a couple of days the apartment smelt like him–which was a comfort. Harrow was just one of those guys who smelt good.

He scattered his stuff all over the guest room: guitar strings, magazines, song sheets, a law quarterly, even a couple of porn books. I read one of them. It's funny how horny those things make you; they're not supposed to but they do. There was one I read, Harrow had underlined it, like it was Kant or Hegel. It was about a school teacher and a naughty student. I read it twice. I wanted to make a copy of it. Anyway.

I went out with the band a couple of times; they got zonked and let me play the drums once. Clayton was gone too but there was a new guy, very friendly, except he had abscesses on his arms. Harrow said it was from too much drumming. Sometimes he was just too fucking much, old Harrow. When he wanted to keep the faith in someone, well, he'd just about have to catch him having sex with an animal before he'd admit that maybe something was a little off.

Then, before I knew it, it wasn't fall anymore. Snow fell on Chinatown. It flickered past the windows sometime during the night and in the morning, down the street, you could hear a shovel scrape against the sidewalk. The sun was very bright that first day.

One cold barren afternoon near the middle of January, I looked out the classroom window. Harrow was standing in the hall, looking uncertainly through the glass. He fanned a pair of fat blue envelopes in the window. They were plane tickets. We were going to Jamaica. Finally.

I tiptoed around. I was sure something was going to wreck it. Illness, a bad tooth, a tax audit, something bad ... it just seemed like too much undeserved fun. I don't know where I got it but I always expect these things to be taken away from me, at the last minute; they never are, but I always wait.

It was our last time together, a goodbye to childhood, a period at the end of a very long sentence.

I didn't go to bed the night before we left. I stayed up, I fussed, I packed a light bag, I put in a couple of my dental brochures to show Harrow. *Power Eating*, I think. A mask, a snorkel, a Mexican switch blade, a T-shirt, a diary, a mickey of vodka. It was as if I were preparing for a performance, not just a holiday. Harrow dropped by around eleven; we went out for a drink, just one. In fact, I put a potato in the oven.

We must have exuded a kind of magnetism that night, because we made a lot of friends. You always do when you're leaving town. We went to an after-hours bar near five in the morning with a couple of Englishmen. Near daylight we got in the car and drove up to our old school. We went in the night-watchman's door; we walked through the halls, we went through the basement lockers, we went into the chapel. When we came out, a winter sun was rising in the sky. Harrow dropped me off at my apartment. Then I remembered the potato. I just about had a fucking heart attack when I did. I ran up the stairs and ripped open the oven. The potato sat inside like a shrunken head. I stared at it incredulously for a moment; someone must have come in and turned it off. But who?

The limo came; I heard the knock downstairs. But that business about leaving the stove on stayed with me all the way to the airport. I know this sounds nuts but I'm pretty good about that stuff. There was a kind of carelessness in it that spooked me.

When did that start, I wondered?

It was a boozy affair from the word go. Not without a certain joy, either. On the way down, fifteen minutes into the flight, I spilt a Bloody Mary on my shirt; it left a violent stain over my heart. Harrow typed on a tiny, old black Remington.

We took a van to Rosemary Cove, stopped by a roadside shack and bought a case of Red Stripe. The driver slapped in a tape and we roared through the thick, potent air. It makes me want to drink, just thinking about it. By the time I got to the hotel, I was hallucinating. We dropped our suitcases into a second-floor room and headed downstairs to the bar.

It was six o'clock in the evening, the sky streaked with violets and blues. We stood at the bar, we ordered ice-cold beers and shots of overproof. A rain-soaked couple from Boston stepped off the road and joined us for a drink.

Someone put on a reggae album. The clouds broke. A golden light passed over the island, over the rich, rain-soaked plants; a breeze blew in from the ocean, a car passed on the road outside.

We headed up the road and turned in at a cliff-side bar. The sun drowned in the ocean. I lay down on a big white lawn chair; I drifted out into the star-soaked night.

"What's the matter with him?" someone said.

I laughed in my sleep. The words never reached my lips. My last memory of the evening is dancing with Harrow at four o'clock in the morning in the red gloom of the Soon Come bar.

When I awoke it was dawn. A dog barked. A rooster crowed. A blood-red light opened like a fan on the horizon. From a hotel down the road, someone played "Imagine." The lyrics floated over the damp dark jungle, over the dogs and the chickens and the roosters and the bloated sleeping bodies. I was so hung over I wanted to weep. I lay on my side, my mouth open, like a wounded animal. I heard Harrow laugh in the darkness.

"Can you imagine how many people have had sex in this room?" he said.

Light spread over the jungle; it seemed to rise from the ground up, to come out of the green, the trees, the roots. Soon a ball of white wax hung over the jungle.

We went down to the bar but it was still closed.

I sat down on the pavement in the shade.

A black boy walked by on the road. It was a beautiful pristine morning. He waved us over. He had fresh mushrooms, wide-brimmed and damp, little Truman Capotes in his hand.

"Magic," the boy said.

Then the grill came up and we went into the bar.

That week I lost five pounds.

I met a beautiful Jewish girl from Des Moines.

I remember a bicycle ride into the hills.

I remember a giant tree poised high over the jungle at sunset.

I remember a starry night.

I had a tiff with a street hustler.

One night, Harrow coaxed a shy boy from his room and brought him out to dinner with us. The kid followed him everywhere.

Some afternoons I heard him typing in his room. I'd peek in the window and there he'd be: cross-legged, typing at the little Remington. Laughing to himself. And taking a plug of white rum.

We were sitting in the hotel bar late one afternoon, the sun fizzling into the sea.

"Boy," Harrow said suddenly, in a tone that rang slightly false, "I'm pooped. I think I'm going to go upstairs for a nap." I stayed downstairs in the bar, reading the *New York Times* and waiting for the Jewish girl to return from her topless sun bath in Bloody Bay. But after a moment or two, I remembered I'd left my wallet in Harrow's room and I nipped across the yard, those skinny dogs following hopefully at my heels, and went up the cement stairs to his room. The door was shut and so I looked in through the grilled window. He was on the phone. I opened the door and stepped into the room. He shot me a furious glance, and raised his hand quickly to silence me. I stared at him bewildered.

"And you were right about the sports jacket," he said eagerly into the phone. I looked at him closely. His brow was wrinkled; a wet, phony smile lay like a damp cloth on his mouth. He was talking to his mother and he looked like a child. I stood motionless. He put his hand over the mouthpiece.

"I don't want her to know you're here," he whispered.

But really, it knocked the shit out of me, the booze, the pills, the late hours. One morning I woke up scared as a rabbit. I tried to have a shower, there was no water pressure, it seemed like an evil portent. Harrow was already up. He sat in the bar, scribbling in a notebook, a Panama hat on his head, a scarf wrapped around his neck, an open flour-sack shirt. His face was slightly grey, sweaty under the eyes but apart from that his energy seemed undiminished. I sat down heavily in the chair opposite him.

"Enough," I said. "Enough pills, enough grass, enough speed, enough liquor."

He put down his pen, threw himself against the back of his chair and clapped his hands with delight.

"I know what you mean," he said. He turned two bloodshot eyes toward me. "I'm slowing down myself." He reminded me of his father in that second.

I went on. "I woke up wanting to weep this morning. You're not supposed to feel like this on your holiday."

I stared out into the woozy heat, the lush vegetation across the road. I shook my head.

"Everything scares me this morning. On the way down here I

was afraid the cleaning lady had taken a real dislike to me."

He looked at me wryly.

"I said hello to her and she didn't acknowledge it. So I bought her off with a towel. I said, when I leave, you can have this towel."

"So what did she say?"

"Nothing, she just nodded."

"It's the hangover," he said. "Makes you jumpy."

At that moment, the couple from Boston poked their heads enthusiastically into the bar. They had settled in, they were relaxed and happy and ready to continue the party they'd stumbled across the first night in town. In fact, they'd come looking for it. My stomach sank when I saw them because I knew what they were expecting. They squeezed in happily beside us. The man had a weak chin. I hadn't noticed it before.

His wife started up: "I told Rod, this place is too quiet, we've got to go and find those two guys."

And then they sat back happily and waited. I said something, they laughed, not because it was funny but because they remembered things being funny. But we were sober now, I was anyway, worse, hung over, and it was agony to think about talking, about the effort required to get it into the air. I felt myself turning inside out from self-consciousness.

The man, sensing something was wrong, looked at me oddly. He was taking it personally.

I didn't want to hurt their feelings; I didn't want to disappoint them. I started in on a funny story but it wasn't working, it wasn't funny, it was strained and acquired a peculiar emphatic bitterness in the retelling. I could feel myself drowning. I stopped and shook my head.

"We're a little hung this morning," Harrow said, coming gently to my defense.

The couple, not understanding, waited. Harrow ordered a beer.

I took a Valium. Then another. I was afraid of starting in on a binge. Harrow popped three in his mouth.

"No point in getting precious now," he said.

I was full of the most awful foreboding.

But soon it faded. Soon I found myself in a druggy, confessional conversation with the woman: about fidelity and love and children and a whole lot of shit I'd said a hundred times before. Fuelled by her approval–and by her husband's expectations, he had a short impatient laugh like a backfire–I had a beer. I thought, well, what the fuck, this is an occasion, this is a reunion, this is a holiday. I looked over at Harrow, like a child, I suppose, looking for him to legitimize the event once again, give it that magic spin. He was sipping gingerly on a pineapple overproof. Look at that, I said to myself, he's already on the hard stuff and *he* can handle it.

So I had a beer, then another. I continued my monologue; at one point my eyes watered up with apparent emotion. I was talking about my son, Jesse. But it wasn't him, of course, it was the pills and the alcohol and the heat and the attention.

A Swede joined us, a muscular, big-boned man. I offered him a beer; he turned it down peremptorily. It left me with an unpleasant sensation. I didn't want him at the table if he wasn't drinking. He seemed, today, irritatingly opinionated and I sensed, or thought I could sense, a ceiling on his intelligence. And it was considerably lower than mine. I realized abruptly what was wrong, why I was seeing the world in such antagonistic hues. I was drinking on an empty stomach. I should eat something, an omelet, yes, a cheese omelet would be good and I ordered one from the waiter who also seemed sullen today, a friend no doubt of the cleaning lady; they'd been talking about me. But by the time the omelet arrived, I had started in on a white rum. The omelet lay to the side in the sweltering heat. I'll eat it in a minute, I thought, I just don't want to wreck my momentum.

The Swede left. A bank teller sat down; he said he wanted to be a fighter pilot.

"Imagine," I said to Harrow, "a bank teller who flies jets." The image undulated with poetic complexity, not to mention the rush of pleasure it gave me to have found so perfect a picture, such succinct, elegant wording. Perhaps my mother was right when she told me I was a poet after all.

Harrow vanished from the table, returned a few moments later with two black capsules of Dexedrine. I took one off-handedly; it was very calculated, my nonchalance. I did it in a manner that suggested I could barely take my attention off what I was saying to pursue the mundane task of taking a pill; whereas in fact my whole attention was absorbed, keyed up for the pill, for it guaranteed a priceless item–continuance. Now with the speed we could go on and on and on....

I confessed again to the woman from Boston; I explained, analyzed some complexity from my life, some key to the miracle of me. In fact I was privately sure she was falling in love with me. How pretty she was too, with chestnut hair falling in curls on to her shoulders, brown eyes. In her fingers she turned a ballpoint pen around and around as she listened.

"Yes," I insisted. "I've been wonderful potential for a long, long time. But school's out. It's been out for years...."

"I guess the speed clicked in," Harrow observed dryly.

"Speed has nothing to do with this," I protested.

"Speed," he said carefully, "has everything to do with it."

And he was right of course. Twenty minutes later, I was lecturing a music teacher from Toronto on mandatory busing, an issue that had been of some significance twenty or thirty years before–in Boston of all places! My, how everything tied in! I spoke with enormous conviction and then never gave the subject another thought.

I moved on. No subject was safe.

"With Beethoven," I said, "it's genius, but you can see how it's done, where it comes from. But with Mozart, it's another story, you have no idea how he gets the things he does. Those Germans, they're geniuses!"

Harrow chewed on a straw and listened, bemused.

The lonely kid from New York wandered out of his room and, drawn to Harrow like an animal toward kindness, lingered at the side of the table until he was invited to sit down.

I ordered another white rum. "I hope I don't smell of this stuff," I said to the woman, raising my head, as it were, for a pat.

"No, no," she said. "No one smells in the tropics." Someone cleared away the omelet.

"Aren't you having a marvellous time?" I said to Harrow.

He nodded.

At that moment, the beautiful Jewish girl walked into the bar. She seemed unsure of herself, lonely, wanting company but not wanting to be perceived that way. She stood at the bar, pretending to ask for directions to a beach hotel. Harrow caught her eye; his arm shot up in a greeting. She smiled quickly but without confidence.

"Alissa," he said, "come sit down."

"Just for a second. I'm meeting friends," she said. It was a rather touching transparency; she was a proud young girl.

She sat beside me. Her arms were bare, I could feel her skin against my arm. I pretended not to notice. By now I had moved on to Samuel Beckett.

The boy from New York had a small weasel-like face, a wispy beard and dark haunted eyes. He couldn't take them off Alissa.

"Alissa," the woman from Boston said, "you've got such beautiful skin, you don't even need to tan."

Alissa lit a cigarette. "They wouldn't let me smoke on the plane," she said.

There was a brief silence at the table.

She asked the waiter for a beer. "In a glass, O.K.? That way I can tell if there's a mousetail in it."

Harrow winced.

A shirtless man in his fifties slippered his way into the bar. He had an effeminate, engaging manner; he was a southerner, and he appeared to know everyone.

"Walter," Harrow said.

He came over. Someone asked how he was.

"Well, Mrs. Patch has got the flu. The Gabriels have the flu. I suppose I'm next." He sat beside Harrow.

"I'll just sit for a bit," he said, looking at each face as he spoke, "then I'm going swimming. It's my only exercise."

The Bostonian, unused to white rum at nine o'clock in the morning, sat slouched in the booth like a stroke victim.

"Do you travel a lot?" Alissa asked the boy. The question thrilled him. His eyes danced with delight and he leaned forward eagerly.

"No," he said. Then added imprudently, "Professional travellers have no soul."

A shadow passed over Alissa's face. Suddenly she understood–the boy had no power within the group, she was wasting her time on him.

He tried again. He started up a conversation with Walter. They were talking about Tolstoy.

"But don't you think that he used up his favourite characters in *War and Peace*?"

There was a hint of gentle ridicule in the boy's voice, as if Walter, because of his manner, his homosexuality, need not be taken seriously. Walter sensed it too.

"No, I certainly do not," he retorted indignantly.

"I don't either," Harrow said gently. He wanted to protect the boy but he too had sensed a rather unpleasant patronizing tone.

"Besides," Walter protested, "those aren't *books*; they're entire *villages*."

I had a minor drunken epiphany. There was a good reason this kid didn't have any friends. He was an asshole.

Alissa frowned. She didn't like this at all. She hadn't read Tolstoy. "He's probably a big fat bore."

A woman in a blue bikini walked by the table.

"You've got a wonderful voice, Walter," the Boston woman said, running a chestnut curl around her finger. "I bet you read a great bedtime story."

He must have had twenty answers to that, but he was a clever man and he left them unsaid. His silence provoked a volley of laughter.

Jamaica opens you up like a fucking can opener and sometime that afternoon I fancied I'd fallen in love with Alissa. She was the daughter of a rabbi, an impossible young woman, breathtakingly self-reverential. Probably very good at parties. She had straight black hair parted in the middle, teeth like Chiclets and dark skin; she looked like an Egyptian beauty. Harrow didn't have five minutes for her; thought she was a spoiled brat.

Later that night, she snuggled against me. Everyone was gone, even Harrow. He went to bed early.

"How are you feeling?" she asked.

I opened my mouth: crows and goblins flew out; she leaned her breasts against my arm. It made my head swim. She was thrilled to have so much effect, it was like a drug. I looked at her, I said God if you give me this girl I'll be good, I'll stop asking for stuff, I promise.

A little while later she took me back to her room, she lit a candle, pulled her shirt over her head and sat on the edge of the bed. I got down on my knees, I've never been so thankful in my life.

I woke her up in the middle of the night to do it again. It was so tender and slow and loving, the curtains rising and falling in puffs of warm air. By morning I was hooked solid.

Which is fine and it sure put a shimmer on the Caribbean; except that night she did the same thing with a German, a German for God's sake. I mean these Jews, don't they have any sense of history? Christ Almighty. It just fucking killed me, I sat transfixed in my chair as if an iron rod had been stuck right through me.

I went to look for Harrow. He was in the bar, scribbling in a notebook.

"Christ," he said. "I hope you're not falling in love with this girl."

"I don't know," I said staring out at the sea.

I tracked her down that night at a dance on the beach. Torches burned on spits in the sand. I asked her if she was going to spend the night with me; she said she didn't know. I persisted; she told me to fuck off.

"I want to have some fun, you know! I don't want to sit in a suffocating room and listen to some guy in his thirties agonize over his life."

"Well, nothing's free," I added ominously.

I wandered off into the music and the lonely tourists.

Harrow found me laid out like a corpse on my mattress the next morning.

"You're not going to give me a lecture, are you?" I said.

"Christ no, I just want to have a drink with someone."

We went down to the bar. I sat by the open window and watched for Alissa to come up the road. I had so many beers Harrow had to help me to my room. By four I was back in the bar, at it again.

And then she came back; it was that gorgeous hour in the Caribbean when a gold light spreads like paint over the island and the water beyond the reefs turns dark and dreamy. She walked up the road alone and came into the bar, sat down, and rested her beautiful head on my shoulder.

"Did you miss me, baby?" she said.

I had a little weep, I told her I'd never been in love before, I said I'd do anything, give her anything, if only she'd go to bed with me. So we went upstairs. Harrow appeared in the middle of it. I was inside her; I stopped moving; I just lay there, it was heavenly. Harrow apologized, he was looking for his playing cards, he said. I think he was laughing. He shuffled through my drawers, through the cupboard. Then he was gone; he shut the door softly.

She vanished again; she went up the road one night. She must have met someone because she didn't come home. I waited like a dog for his master. But no luck.

The next day, I wanted to punish her. I wanted to vanish forever and make her miss me. Harrow and I rented motorcycles and headed across the island. I had to get out of town. It was the only way I could stay away from her.

We rode through brilliant little towns, we waved like emperors at ragged children who scrambled from houses to see us. We ran alongside the sea. The sun burned our wrists, we stopped under a giant tree. Harrow clambered off his bike and wandered out over a bed of volcanic lava; he walked carefully, right to the very edge, and peered down into the sea. I gave my camera to a child to snap a picture. I still have it. Harrow is wearing sunglasses, a straw hat tied to his head like a bonnet, and his flour-sack shirt. Two strong legs emerge from shorts. Beside him I look thin and crooked. I look preoccupied. I must have been thinking about Alissa.

She came back, that day or the next. She stayed with me all night, but then she was gone again in the morning; someone said they saw her on a yacht. I should have given it up. I tried, but I couldn't. Her presence induced a kind of paralysing self-consciousness. I could barely get out a sentence.

Then suddenly it was our last night in town. I figured I owed it to Harrow so I slipped my lead early in the afternoon and didn't go back to the hotel. I imagined her looking for me everywhere. We went out and got stoned; ate a mess of mushrooms in an omelet. Got higher than kites. The world bristled with clever innuendo, double entendre. Darkness fell; a round moon soared into the sky. Gales of laughter blew us down the road. Weak-kneed with laughter, Harrow leaned against a banyan tree and scribbled in his notebook. Suddenly, out of nowhere, there was Alissa. She had tracked us down. I followed her meekly back to the hotel, Harrow a few steps behind me. He was getting tired of this and I didn't blame him.

We went up to his room; we sat outside on the terrace, right at the very edge, hanging over the jungle. Moonlight poured down. In the distance a tree rose high, high up against the starry sky. Voices drifted across the bay from a big hotel. Music. A car passed. Then there was the sound of sandals on cement. Alissa stood beside my chair, her profile to me. She felt me looking at her but I didn't turn away; I ached to take her in my arms, to love her unprotectedly. Harrow cleared his throat. I laughed.

"What?" Alissa said.

She wore a white Mexican shirt. It fell like moonlight over her breasts.

"I think I'd like a beer," Harrow said hoarsely, as if he hadn't spoken for some time.

"I'll get it," I said. I got up, sweat trickled down my chest, it trickled under my arms, but it was erotic; dizzyingly carnal. I started down the stairs. Alissa sat in the chair beside Harrow. "Me too," she said. "A beer for me too." It united them, those two beers.

I heard her chair squeak, as if she were getting up. I got to the bottom of the stairs. A small, ugly dog ran up to me. His collar rattled. I jumped with fright. Then I bent down to pat him. I looked up at the balcony. There was no sound, I could see nothing. But the silence. They weren't talking. I stood at the bottom of the balcony.

"Did you say you wanted a beer?" I called up from the shadows.

Silence, then a girl's laughter.

"Yes," she said. I was sure I heard it, a faint mocking in her voice. I walked across the lawn, past the dartboard. Moths whirled around a lamp in the driveway, I could suddenly hear the sea, then a boy's voice from the bar. I was coming into the light, something starting to spin in my stomach, a kind of urgency as if I was late for something and getting later, seriously, dangerously late. I passed a couple sitting on the stairs. They sat still as a painting. I went into the bar. The owner was sitting at a table with three cronies. A bottle of white rum sat in the centre of the table. They talked, they interrupted, they exploded with the laughter of men who are drunk and talking about things that happened twenty years before. I waited by the bar. I was invisible.

Finally I said, "Excuse me."

They didn't hear me. Then one said, "Junior, junior," and poked at the owner's elbow. He rose leisurely, still laughing, straightening his pants, and came behind the bar.

"Mr. Blackwood," he said and then, for no apparent reason, laughed. But that laugh, too, unsettled me. It was as if he were in on the joke, as if overnight I had become the hotel pet. I was also aware of making an effort to keep a lid on something, something that was pushing back.

He opened the cooler, looked over at his chums, laughed again, called something in patois. Then he took a bottle opener and thoughtfully, remembering something else, uncapped the bottles, one by agonizing one.

"All right, Christian," he said and I was free. Just as I stepped into the yard, it engulfed me, a most awful, hysterical panic, like a child who has lost sight of his mother on a busy street. I hurried across the grass, the beer spilt on my hands, I ran up the stairs and stepped on to the terrace, into the moonlight. Alissa sat on Harrow's lap, her arm draped on his shoulder. My feet pushed me forward. Harrow didn't look at me. His face was in shadow. I put a beer on the floor beside his chair. I couldn't move. I just stood there.

I heard a sound I didn't recognize. It was like a sigh. Was he already inside her? Was it a groan of pleasure? Harrow muttered something into her ear. I couldn't make it out.

"What?" she said, softly, like a lover.

Then he said it again.

"You're going to have to get up," he said in a voice flat as cement. "You're a bit heavy."

With a hollow laugh, she got up; her arm fell from his shoulder.

"I'm pooped," he said. "Time for my jammies."

I could have got up and cheered. I could have thrown my arms around him and hugged him.

He shuffled off to his room, I could hear his feet dragging theatrically on the cement. To this day I can't think of that moment without smiling, without feeling an almost physical sensation of affection for Harrow.

I sat there a while longer. Then Alissa said, "What?"

I waited a moment. I knew what it would cost me but I said it anyway.

"You're a real asshole, Alissa," I said.

And then she too was gone and I was alone in the moonlight.

Chapter Seven

We didn't see each other for some time after we got back to Toronto. At first I thought it was because we'd seen enough of each other for a while, but then, after six weeks, I called him at home. There was no answer. I left a message on the service, but he never got back to me. A couple of weeks later, I tried him at his mother's house but when I heard her voice, a kind of anxiety, fright I suppose, seized me and I put down the phone. I wasn't in the mood to talk to someone who despised me. It left a bad aftertaste, a jangle, like a dog that has frightened you in the street.

Perhaps that was it. I wondered if I was still frightened of her. There was still a part of me, a child, who responded to that cold, harrowing voice. Something else odd: I had the feeling she knew it was me. That she put down the phone and said to someone in the room, "That was Christian."

Then one Friday afternoon the phone rang. I had just got back from school. It was Harrow. He was at his house in Callington.

"Why don't you come up here for the weekend," he said. "I'd love to see you."

"How do I recognize the place?" I said.

"It looks like the house in *Psycho*," he said and hung up.

It was late that afternoon when I left Toronto. I took my motorcycle. I thought it might be an exhilarating ride, the rolling blue-line roads, the country air, the smell of fresh grass growing. It was early May, but I wasn't on the road twenty minutes before the sun disappeared behind the clouds. I got a chill and with it came a sense of foreboding. I pulled into a restaurant and ate bacon and eggs and hot coffee. My hands were shaking; the coffee cup rattled against the saucer. A grizzled farmer in a baseball hat watched me. He didn't understand why I was shaking.

Back out on the road, the cold air blew up my sleeves, the sky grew sinister, leaden. A kind of ennui filled me. I started up a long patch of highway. A church steeple rose at the end. It seemed to take forever, I seemed to be standing still; the wind pushed me to one side, then to the other. A truck came up behind me but I was daydreaming and I didn't hear it until it roared by. I jumped with fright; the handlebars swerved, the tail wind sucked me to the side of the road, I veered along the edge of the pavement, only inches from the gravel shoulder. I held my breath and I waited for the impact. The bike danced along a ribbon of grey as I leaned away from the embankment; and then gradually the bike moved back toward the centre line.

I pulled off the road. I got off the bike and went down and sat in a field. My heart was beating so hard I saw stars. I waited until I calmed down; I could feel the cold earth through the seat of my pants. Smell wet grass. Hear the wind blowing over the field.

Then I rode on. But I couldn't shake the sensation that something bad was going to happen. I drove for forty minutes through the grey countryside; the trees were bare, there were no buds, no leaves, the grass lay in colourless mounds in the fields.

I pulled into a small town and called him from a corner grocery store. I had such a bad chill my voice was shaking.

"Go through town for a mile, take a gravel laneway on the left; it's the third farmhouse. It looks like the house in *Psycho*."

It worried me, this repetition.

I rode gingerly along a narrow gravel road. A solitary man raised his arm in the middle of a field and waved in my direction. He waved only once and then turned sharply and disappeared into a red brick farmhouse.

It was a tall house; it leaned forward as if its spine were broken. I rolled in the driveway. Harrow emerged from the screened side door and came down the stairs. He was wearing a long raincoat. He was pale. He had a bottle of mineral water in his hand. Something was wrong. I could tell.

We went into the house. I couldn't stop shaking.

"Let me go and get you a sweater," he said and disappeared into the bedroom. I got a glimpse after him. A mattress lay on the floor.

It was a lovely old farmhouse, hardwood floors, high ceilings, big windows. A modern kitchen, black-and-white tile floor, an electric stove. He came out with a grey sweater.

"It's brand new," he said. "My mother bought it for me last week. She lives just down the road."

He offered me a beer. I took it. I sat on the kitchen counter. He had a beer too.

"You look pale," I said.

"Sure. Fine."

"Are you stoned?"

"No."

We finished the beer. He took me into his study which ran off the kitchen. Bookshelves lined the wall, rows and rows of books, hardbacks and paperbacks, I recognized titles from university: *The Golden Bough, Anatomy of Criticism*; a row of bright Scribner titles, Thomas Wolfe, Hemingway, Ring Lardner, Fitzgerald, all beautifully intact, the spines unbroken. He looked after his things, Harrow, he always had. Walt Whitman in several editions. *The Little Prince.*

Below the bay window, a beautiful work desk, dark, moist-feeling wood. A rich red leather chair faced the desk. It spoke of privilege and a practised appetite for comfort. A single-barrelled shotgun leaned against the wall. In the corner, a row of black guitar cases, like coffins, six, seven, maybe more; a battery of gleaming tape recorders, all Sonys. A spear from Jamaica on the wall. I remembered it from his bedroom in Forest Hill.

"It's a great place," I said. "You've always got great places."

He nodded. There was a grimness, a gravity, about him that I couldn't place. He didn't seem drunk, I couldn't smell anything; he wasn't a dope smoker, he said very little so he wasn't on speed, it didn't feel spacy, like acid, I couldn't place it. And it wasn't downers because he was clearheaded and precise in the way he walked, went around corners. At one point a piece of sheet music slipped off a table and he reached over and caught it in mid-air. No, he certainly wasn't on downers. But he was so fucking pale, so serious, I wondered. The sense of foreboding grew. I had a second beer but I couldn't touch the chill. It made me shake, I could hear it in my voice.

We were back in the kitchen. I was sitting on the counter, Harrow in a rocking chair. He held a beer bottle at an angle, almost allowing it to spill, not quite. Suddenly there was a noise outside; it was the crunch of stones under the wheels of a car. I looked at Harrow. His eyebrows went up. Harrow got out of the rocker and looked out the window. He put down his beer quickly. I don't know why but I lowered my head. I could feel something odd getting a grip on me, my heart started to pound and my stomach tightened. I heard the screen door open, I heard the glass door open and then I heard her voice. I didn't look up. She exchanged quiet greetings with her son. I looked up.

"Is that Christian Blackwood?" she said in a syrupy, sickly sweet voice.

There it was again: the sensation of being a child in the presence of a powerful adult who despises you. The sudden, pounding heart, the damp hands.

"Hello, Florence," I said.

It was as if a switch had been flicked. Her mouth was seized by a gleaming, involuntary smile. She blinked quickly. Her thoughts appeared to have locked in their haste to find a suitable, possible punishment for this insolence. She didn't like me calling her by her first name. I saw her cut down a maid once for the same thing.

"Florence is it now?" she said.

It didn't satisfy either of us. I'd had enough of this stuff, these scare-the-kiddy shenanigans.

Regaining herself–she didn't want to seem so *affected*–she crossed the room briskly, her hand extended. But I was warming to the occasion.

"I don't want to shake hands with you, Florence."

"I see," she said. She withdrew her hand and turned away quickly.

Harrow scowled.

I slipped down off the counter and went into the bathroom. I didn't have to pee. I wanted to be alone, to relish a childhood victory, the settling of an old score. I sat on the toilet, I vibrated with excitement. A worm in my heart worked itself free and passed away into my blood stream.

I put on a very solemn face, as if at a funeral, and emerged from the bathroom. They were in the driveway. Harrow was explaining something. His mother had her lips pressed together, she was furious, she shot a glance at the window where I was standing and the sheer electricity, the hatred, made me step back. She got in her Thunderbird. Harrow leaned over and gave her an obedient peck on the cheek. I watched the car drive down the driveway, turn right and head off up the road, dust rising behind it.

Then Harrow came in.

"You really despise each other, don't you?"

I chose the words carefully.

"Oh, I don't know," I said casually. "I think despise is too strong a word for it."

"I've got to buy some hamburger buns," he said. I knew he was lying, that he was going to his mother's.

Night fell. I grew bored waiting for him to return and I began to browse through the house.

Under a shelf in the corner I discovered a scrapbook in which Harrow had pasted his favourite nudie photos. The glue, the cutting out, the pasting, it felt like a child's project. It was hard core, pouting girls with whips, ejaculating cocks.

I opened a drawer in his desk. Shotgun shells roamed carelessly. A passport, heavily stamped–Ethiopia, South Africa, France. Sheaves of writing in Harrow's hand. There were dozens and dozens of pages, single spaced, not a line taken out or corrected. I read a paragraph: bad Walt Whitman. Underneath was a clear plastic bag whose contents looked like cocaine, except darker, slightly grey, and rockier. How banal, I thought, how stunningly, unforgivably banal. Doing coke and lying about it. That was why he looked so dreadful, that explained the manic hobbying, the scrapbook ... a rich boy in the country with a big bag of coke and nothing to do.

I took the bag out of the drawer and opened it up. Took a sniff. I put a crumb on my thumb and rubbed it against my gum. The taste was appalling. It filled my mouth with a kind of metallic foulness. It was something synthetic. Methedrine maybe. Uppers. But not coke, that was certain. For a moment I thought of throwing it out, but I hesitated. I imagined Harrow coming home, looking for his little white bag. Flying into a rage because he couldn't find it, crashing into my room.

I went to the kitchen and opened a beer. It was after nine and I was getting tired. I had a nasty feeling that Mrs. Winncup would be back. She couldn't let it go at that.

I yawned. The telephone rang. I let it ring. The answering machine clicked in. A crude voice came over the speaker.

"Harrow, this is Jimmy." Then a stupid laugh, self-conscious and stoned.

"Give me a call, buddy." I stared out the window. Who *were* these assholes? They were always around.

I could see the lights of the farmhouse half a mile away across the dark field.

The phone rang again. I thought it was Harrow, but instead a woman's voice came on. It was Zinta; she sounded calm and self-possessed.

"I got your message," the voice said. "You shouldn't leave that stuff on my machine. My sister comes over to water the plants occasionally."

What was that? A dirty message? Harrow was talking dirty on the phone now? What the fuck was going on? It made me sleepy, all of it.

I put my feet on the desk. I leaned my head back. I looked up at the ceiling. Written in a small, feminine script were the words *I love you.*

Soon, the beer, the exhaustion from the ride, the visit from Florence, it all caught up to me; it engulfed me in a giant, eye-watering yawn that almost sent me careening backwards. The house was so wonderfully quiet; even the fridge had clicked off; there wasn't a sound. Not a peep anywhere. No wind, nothing. I pulled down my feet, got up.

I lay in the guest bedroom on the second floor. Soon I fell asleep. I had a hideous dream. I was wandering in a garden behind a mansion. It was a gloomy, melancholy spring day. Near the bottom of the garden was a wooden shed and from it an angry voice hissed. "Just you wait, mister, I'll get you."

It was Florence Winncup's voice.

Near three in the morning I heard footsteps downstairs. I was going to get up but I was so tired, my limbs so heavy they felt drugged. Later, just after daylight, I heard steps again. I looked at the clock. It was 6:30. He was still up. What could he possibly be up to?

When I awoke again, it was after ten in the morning. I had a bad headache. I came downstairs and into the kitchen. Harrow was sitting at the table. He looked almost green with ill health. A radio played in the study.

"Have you got something for a hangover?" I asked. He gave me a wry smile.

"I sure do."

He went into the study, opened the bottom drawer and came back with the bag.

"What's that?" I said.

"China White."

He laid out a line on the table and chopped it up with a razor. Deft, delicate little strokes. His blunt fingers were well-groomed; they looked like a doctor's fingers.

"What is it?" I asked again.

"This stuff," he said, "will make a hangover afraid of *you.*"

He rolled up a dollar bill and stuck it in his nose and took a snort. "You'll love it."

"It's not going to kill me, is it?"

"No, Christian, it won't."

"Are you sure this is what I need for a hangover? I was thinking of an aspirin."

"Don't fight me on this one."

I bent over and took a snort. It seared my nose, made my eyes water, slipped down the back of my throat like rusty mucus.

"Nothing happened," I said.

"Wait."

"Is it like junk?"

"You'll see."

"The funny thing about junk is that it used to make me feel very industrious."

"I haven't done junk since law school," Harrow said.

"Me neither," I said. "But you know, Harrow, this tastes like gun-barrel shavings. Very synthetic. Sort of wicked. Unhealthy."

"I love it. It's made me stupider, I think, but I love it."

We were silent for a moment. His chair creaked.

"I don't think I got off," I said.

He diced up a small rock into four lines of dirty white powder and we did another snort. Just as I inhaled, my stomach turned over in protest.

Suddenly, the radio dominated the room. "The year is 1964," the D.J. announced, "and this song was number one in the nation."

Then we heard those familiar, rushing chords; bright cheerful voices burst into the kitchen like sunlight.

Close your eyes and I'll kiss you
Tomorrow I'll miss you. . . .

"My mother always liked this song," I said. "But I've always found something rather dull right at the heart of it."

"No hook."

"What?"

"It doesn't have a hook. A middle eight."

"A very feeble one anyway."

"I like the hook in 'This Boy,'" he said. "When he goes way high up like that . . . "

He leaned forward. "My mother didn't like the Beatles," he said. "She thought they were selfish."

"Shellfish?"

"Selfish!"

"Oh. Selfish."

I got up and got a glass of water, leaving what appeared to be a trail of fire behind me.

"I just scorched my hangover," I said. "A scorched-earth policy vis-à-vis the old hangover."

I came back and sat down, my hand still wrapped around the glass. I took a sip, even though I was not thirsty, then another. It gave me something concrete to do, an identifiable activity in a roomful of shifting possibilities.

The D.J. broke in breathlessly.

"You may have heard that George, Paul, Ringo and Julian have got together in the studio. What we have here in fact is a

Beatles reunion!"

Harrow got up and disappeared into the study; the radio cut out; he came back. I stared out the window. A plane passed soundlessly overhead. I followed its course across the blue sky. Suddenly, the room jumped; then slowly, like jelly on the wall, slid downwards. My stomach turned.

"I don't feel very well," I said.

At the side of my vision, the furniture in the room was in a constant state of aggravated motion: chairs skeetered, carpets retreated. Snapping my head around, everything crashed to a guilty halt; then slowly, naughtily, a different portion of the room, again just out of sight, jumped gleefully into motion.

My stomach turned again. My heart thumped. It beat like a horse cantering sideways toward death.

"Am I in any danger here?" I asked.

"From me?"

"From the drug." I inhaled deeply and continued. "Because if I am, tell me and I'll go to the hospital."

Harrow put his hands behind his head and stared out the window at the screaming green fields.

"I feel like something terrible is going to happen," I said.

He didn't respond.

Outside the cicadas buzzed sleepily.

The only way out of this, I thought slowly, is to think my way out. But how can I think my way out when it's my thinking that got me here? Start again. I've got to stop thinking like this. But the thing that's realizing that the thinking is bad is the very thing that's doing the thinking. I could feel myself slipping into a dangerous spin. But I couldn't leave it alone. All right. The camera's fucked. It's taking bad pictures. Don't try to figure out what's wrong with the pictures by using the camera that took them....

So forget the pictures. Until you get your camera fixed.

Fine, but what until then?

Borrow someone else's camera.

I looked at Harrow.

But his camera is more fucked than mine. God knows what his pictures look like. Here's a solution. Go ahead and take pictures. Just ignore them.

But how can I ignore them? They're the only ones I've got.

I got up and went outside on to the porch. It was lovely out there, sunny, the fields were yellow and rolling in the morning sun. A tractor puttered across the horizon. Dandelions, hundreds and hundreds of dandelions dotted the grass. I drifted out into the middle of the field and sat down. The sun poured down, poured over my face like sticky honey. I felt white and sick. A white fluffy cloud stood in a blue sky; it was like a child's drawing. It made me suddenly ache for my son, ache for his smell, his small hands on my face. I wondered suddenly if I was going to die out there in that dandelion-dotted field, roll over and die like a scarecrow, the wind shuffling my clothes. How I would miss him. How I would miss watching him grow up. How could I have jeopardized all that, just for this, just to get stoned one more time? I was going to die out here in this sun-washed field and I'd never see him again. My heart was going to go tick tick and then it was just going to stop.

The screen door opened and Harrow started across the grass toward me.

"Don't ignore me on this one, Harrow. Am I in any danger here? Just tell me and I'll go to the hospital."

He popped a blade of grass in his mouth.

"What are you so frightened of?"

"I just am."

I touched his coat sleeve. But he ignored me. He took off his jacket, then unbuttoned his shirt and took it off too. I stared at him speechless. He stood up and dropped his pants, then stepped out of his underwear. Stark naked, his hands pressed together, he sat in the dandelion field and began to pray.

Our Father who art in heaven
Hallowed be thy name, . . .

"Harrow," I said.

Thy kingdom come
Thy will be done, . . .

"Harrow," I whispered, "listen! Please! Don't do this. Not now. Am I in any danger here? Should I go to the hospital? Am I in danger?"

He turned a colourless face toward me.

"You are unless you pray with me."

He rolled over in a somersault, then another. He was doing them in a circle around me, his bottom opening and closing in my face, the weeds and the loose grass sticking to his grey flesh. In the flat, cold sunshine, I saw him suddenly as a kind of obscene larva rolling over and over in the grass. It was a picture that I could feel, could smell actually searing on to my imagination. I can still see it. I wish I couldn't but I can.

He glared at me, black eyed.

"You don't take me seriously, do you?"

Then he got up and walked slowly, unselfconsciously back inside. The whole thing had taken two minutes, maybe three. When he came out a few minutes later, he was dressed. He stood by the car.

"Come on," he said, "let's go."

I went over. "Harrow," I began, "I don't feel very well. I don't think I'm up for a trip to town."

"Suit yourself," he said crisply. He got in the car, started the engine, then rolled the window down.

"Say," he said, as if thinking his way through the sentence. "When you see my mother . . . "

He paused.

"Yes?" I said.

"Ask her to forgive you."

He backed the car up across the dandelion field and glided down the driveway. He turned on to the road and I watched him drive along the horizon till he was gone. I stood for a moment on that hot driveway, the stones and the gravel shining in the sun and then I went into the house.

I lay down on the couch; I watched the ceiling curl at the edges like burning love letters. I went upstairs and got a sheet and a pillow and I brought them back down into the study. I couldn't stand to be up there, it was too lonely, too much like a deathbed. I laid the pillow on the couch. I took off my shirt, my skin was prickly hot and I lay down on the couch, covered my chest with a fresh sheet and stared up at the ceiling, repeating never again, never again. Just the sound of my own voice comforted me. I tried not to listen to my heart, I thought it would make it self-conscious, might make it stop.

"It's the camera," I said out loud. "The camera's fucked." I imagined my mother's cool hand on my forehead.

Then a car pulled up outside. I laid a hand over my forehead. Footsteps clattered like an insect across the floor and the door flew open.

It was Florence Winncup. She had come back for round two. She looked haggard and furious.

"You're still here!" she said. "Why are you still here?"

She hovered in the door. I thought she might attack me, scratch my face, strike me with a poker. I wanted to level with her, to appeal to the mother in her, to tell her, look, I've taken a terrible drug, I'm frightened and sick, I'm not up for this now. You've got to be kind to me. Maybe I'd burst into tears, show her I meant it. But better sense got me. This was not a woman to trust, not with that information, not with being weak. In fact, none of them was trustworthy, not Harrow either. I had no business being near any of them.

I stared at Florence.

"Go away," I said. Her heels clattered across the tile floor, she was dying to find her son, to report a fresh insult. The car took off.

A squirrel ran across the telephone line outside the house. Maybe that squirrel, I thought, maybe that squirrel can save me from all this sordidness. I thought of getting up and getting on my motorcycle but I was too rattled, too stoned. I saw a picture of myself, paralysed in a wheelchair, body ruined, all because I was frightened of Florence, had let her drive me out of the house before I was straight enough to drive. No, I wasn't going to do that. And yet I was scared to be in the house, that she would get to Harrow first, tell him lies, tell him I'd struck her. Fire him up, make him violent. A wave of fresh fear touched my heart, made it kick up again. God, just get me up, get me out of here. But I couldn't go. Couldn't get on the bike yet.

I got up and went to the bathroom. My face sheened. The room filled with nightmare bright light. God forgive me, I said, God forgive me. I looked at the clock. It was two in the afternoon. Cicadas hummed in the grass, the hum soared up like a cloud. On a back clothesline, a sleeping bag hung still in the windless day. Down the road, I saw a boy come out of the back of his farmhouse and lie down in a hammock. He wore a white T-shirt. He looked so young, so healthy, so languid on that beautiful summer's day. I could taste metal in my mouth like a rusty knife. I could feel rusty blood running through my veins. I felt like a very, very old car that was parked on a cliff and was going to give one more kick, then tumble into the canyon, into the white water and green trees and healthy young buds. I'd crash down through the cracking branches and the breaking limbs.

I don't know how long I lay there; I felt the day grow cool, saw the shadows lengthen from the forest. Then I heard a car. I got up and peeked out the window. It was Harrow. At long last Harrow. I forgot myself momentarily, my need to protect myself from him. I went to the front door and, wrapped in a sheet, stood on the porch. The car stopped. The door opened. Harrow got out and gave a little hop, a joyful little hop, like someone who wants to be taken back, forgiven for being "a character."

I watched him from the doorway. Then the other door opened. Pascal Charleville got out.

"Pascal!" a white-faced Harrow shrieked and pointed at me.

"Look who's here!" Pascal reached into the car and pulled out a flute. Then the two of them were in the driveway, the shadows spreading across the field, Harrow dancing like a circus bear and Pascal tooting on his silver flute.

Pascal ducked into the car and emerged with a cassette in his hand.

"Harrow," he said, "there's a song here I'm going to die if I don't hear."

Harrow wrinkled up his brow. He knew I was making up my mind, that if he brought Pascal into the house, I was leaving.

"Sure," he said and stepped aside.

I went into the house and got dressed, picked my motorcycle keys off the kitchen table. Harrow caught me going out.

"Where are you going?" he said. "We're just about to have a barbecue."

"I have to go, Harrow," I said.

"Really?" He looked serious for a second.

"Your colour is not good," I said.

"I need some exercise," he said. He patted his tummy. "I need to drop twenty."

"The China White is terrible stuff. You should flush it down the toilet."

"Maybe you're right."

I threw a leg over my motorcycle.

"By the way, your mother came by."

"Really?" he said.

Harrow looked out at yellow Van Gogh fields and smiled almost privately.

"All these comings and goings, it'd make a great play. Maybe I'll write it all down."

"I'll see you, Harrow," I said. I started up the bike and ran it slowly down the driveway. I knew that things would never be the same for us again, that in a way, once and for all, my childhood was over.

I rode the long way back to Toronto; it took me three or four hours. I was still stoned and I stayed on little roads, right near the side. When I got home it was just before nightfall, the sky a sad pink, the smell of spring in the air, a star twinkled just above the horizon. I went upstairs and had a bath, brushed my teeth, washed my hair, read the newspaper in the tub, then called up the little boy. I wanted his soul, his body, to heal me.

I lay down on my bed. I listened to the sounds of a spring night in the city. There was a level of excitement, of keenness to the voices. Like children let out to play after dark.

I rolled over, turned over my pillow, closed my eyes. Sleep came down like snow.

It was still dark when the phone rang. The ring woke me up like a gunshot. My stomach knotted, I felt nauseated. I couldn't remember why I felt so nightmarishly ill. Did I have a hangover? Then I remembered. The phone rang again. I wondered about the little boy.

"Yes," I said, leaning over the bed, holding the black phone in my hand. I could feel the blood rush to my head.

There was a long, long pause on the phone.

"Harrow," I whispered.

I could hear breathing.

"Harrow," I said.

Then the line clicked dead.

"Fucking asshole," I said to the dark room and went back to sleep. I woke up again to a bright, sunshiny Saturday morning. Down the street someone played a piano. I went into the kitchen; the sun played on the stone face of the booby hatch across the street. The place looked downright cheerful today, as if heads might pop from the windows and burst into song. I remembered the phone call. I'd have to speak to Harrow about that. Tell him not to call a parent at five o'clock in the morning. But I wouldn't be seeing Harrow for some time.

I made a cup of coffee, went out to buy the paper, took it down the hall, sat in the foyer overlooking the street. I was still shaky.

The phone rang. I picked it up and waited. I said nothing.

"It's me," said a flat voice finally.

"Harrow?" I said.

"Yes."

"Was that you last night?"

"Last night?" I knew he was about to tell a lie. I was tired of it, tired of him.

"What's up?" I said.

"Can you come up here?" he said.

"No, I can't."

"Please."

"No. Can't do it, Harrow. Got a full day."

There was a long pause.

"You've got to come here." It was a blank, unselfconscious statement, like the unblinking look from a dying man. It asserted no power, but it feared nothing.

"What's up?"

"Look, please, you've got to come here."

"I'm too old for surprises, Harrow. And you should know not to call people at five o'clock in the morning."

"If you never do anything I ask again, fine, but please come here now."

"What's happened."

"I can't say."

"Don't be coy, Harrow."

He didn't answer.

"Is Pascal there?"

"No."

"Don't tell me a whopper now."

"No, he's not." He was telling the truth. I knew it. I put down the phone. I got on my motorcycle, I drove along the main highway, it got me there faster. I drove up the long stretch of road with the church at the end. It was shorter today, warmer, the trip didn't take so long and by the time I was puttering along the country road, the sun was shining, the flowers, the dandelions swayed in the fields. I turned on to the dirt road. Harrow was sitting in front of his house. His back to a tree. I stopped the bike. He didn't get up. I walked over to him. He shaded his eyes from the sun. He was smiling. He had a bottle of mineral water on his lap.

"A little dehydrated?" I said.

He got up.

"I've done something terrible," he said.

He took me into the house. A patch of kitchen floor tiles had been torn up. We went into the study; the floor was littered with books. A guitar lay on its back, the neck snapped off. It was cherry red. An unfamiliar shotgun lay on the floor. Something gleamed on the wall. A bottle of Remy Martin lay empty on its side on the carpet. There was a funny smell in the air, I couldn't place it, it reminded me of something a long time ago. It teased my memory.

Harrow led me through the study. I stepped over the Jamaican spear. He opened the side door and stepped into the backyard. I followed him. Nearby in a rusted oil drum, something foul smouldered, it smelled like burning rubber. Harrow pointed to something leaning against the house. It was covered in a sleeping bag. He went over.

"This isn't very pleasant," he said. He pulled back the bag. A bug crawled along the wound in the forehead. The blood was black, coagulated. It was Pascal.

"Jesus," I said and my body, independent of me, took a jump backwards. I glanced again at him.

"Jesus."

There was a very peculiar look on Harrow's face. It was serious, but only on the surface. As if he were waiting to see my response before he let me see his. It reminded me of my brother the day Father died, when he opened the door of his apartment, waiting to see how I expected him to be.

So, out of nerves, I laughed, a strange laugh that sounded alien even to my ears and bent my mouth in a funny shape. I had a feeling it looked very unattractive.

"Pascal Charleville paid the ultimate price for messing up my room," Harrow said.

I went over to the body and bent over and looked at the face. The eyes were closed. I reached over and touched his neck. The skin felt cold, it had the texture of porcelain and sand.

"Is he dead?"

"As a doornail," Harrow said.

"What happened?"

"I shot him."

"I can see that, Harrow."

The body rumbled. I jumped back.

"It's just gas," Harrow said. "He's done that before."

"Where are his clothes?"

"In there," Harrow said, nodding toward the smouldering barrel.

"You burned his clothes?"

"I tried. They wouldn't catch." He went over and peered in the barrel. A large, cheerfully coloured can of barbecue fluid sat beside the drum.

"I'd plug him again if I had to," he said.

"That's an unfortunate turn of phrase, Harrow. I hope you'll avoid it when you talk to the police."

He looked at me with a look of dark irony.

"I'm not going to call the police."

"Harrow," I began.

"I'm going to chop him up and burn him."

Harrow threw the cover back over the body.

"Harrow," I said quietly, "this is very serious."

"Damn straight it's serious," he said. I'd never heard him use that expression.

"You can't chop him up, Harrow."

"No one knows he's here. He's got no friends. It'll be like it never happened."

"Where did you pick him up?"

"At his mother's. But she wasn't there. No one was."

"Did you stop anywhere on the way out here?"

"No. Yes. For gas. Doesn't matter."

"Can we just go inside and talk about this?"

"All right, but I don't have all day."

We sat in the kitchen. He pulled down a nearly full bottle of rye and poured himself a shot.

"Do you think it's a good idea to have liquor on your breath when the police come?"

"I told you. The police aren't coming."

He gazed at me, a long, coolly appraising look, as if to say unless you're going to call them, that is.

He poured me a shot. I let it stand in front of me.

"What happened, Harrow?" I said. "You guys seemed to be having such fun." The words sounded inane.

"It was the Remy Martin. He came in and swiped it off the top of the counter and drank half of it. Like that. Then he did the big switcheroo."

His choice of words was, to say the least, peculiar, more so because he was using the language of my mother, of his mother, words and phrases from a generation before.

"What switcheroo?" My mouth distorted again into that unattractive smile.

"Mean."

"Mean? How so?"

"Pulling down books, throwing them around the room, wrecking the place . . . "

"That's not why you shot him, is it, for wrecking your stuff?"

He looked peevish suddenly, like a cornered, lying child.

"Look, I don't have time for this."

"So what happened? He wrecked a couple of books."

"A couple of books!" Harrow shrieked incredulously. "Look at this mess. Look at what he did to my guitar." I was suddenly aware of how audible silence was. You could actually hear it, the sound of compressed air, with a slight ring to it.

Harrow forced himself to speak calmly. His voice dropped an octave. It was as if he had made a decision about how to handle me.

"Did he threaten you?" I asked.

"Yes. Yes, of course he threatened me," he said softly. I

believed that. I knew Harrow well enough to know that he must have been in authentic danger, must have at least *believed* himself to be in real danger before he fired. Even stoned, he wouldn't have got that wrong.

"How did he threaten you?"

"Yeah, with the guitar. He had it cocked on his shoulder like an axe. I thought he was going to bean me with it." The word *bean* made him smile, although he didn't realize quite why.

"Did you have the gun?"

"Yes, I'd just picked it up."

"Was it loaded?"

"Yep. I picked it up and cracked it open and put a shell in the chamber."

"Where were you standing?"

"By the desk."

"All right, go on. Where was he?"

"In front of the leather chair."

"So what happened?"

"I said, 'Pascal, put down the guitar.'"

"And you pointed the gun at him."

"Yeah."

"And it went off."

"No, no, no." He shook his head as if I were confusing him.

"He smashed the guitar, see, it shattered there, against the doorway."

He pointed to an indentation in the wall. Then I knew what the smell was in the study. It was gunpowder in a closed room. Once when I was thirteen Harrow and I had fired my dad's deer rifle out the back window in Forest Hill. It had made a dreadful, end-of-the-world bang, torn a hole in the backyard tree, rattled the windows and left this sharp smell in my bedroom.

There was a shiny stain on the wall.

"What's that?" I said.

"Don't ask."

"What is it?"

"That's where his brains landed."

I looked back at him.

"Go on," I said evenly.

"He smashed the guitar against the wall; I didn't plug him for that, although I wanted to," he said with sudden energy, as if he'd found suddenly a solid patch of the truth, like cement, underneath his feet.

"You've got to stop using that word."

"Then he reached up and grabbed the spear. I put the gun to my shoulder, I cocked it this time and said, 'Pascal, put down the motherfucking spear.' He said, 'You're a goner,' and then he cocked his arm back like this." With excessive concentration, Harrow drew his arm back. Was there something slightly mechanical, slightly recited, that I'd just noticed? I wasn't sure.

"So he was going to throw the spear at you?"

"Damn straight."

"Stop saying that. It's schizophrenic. So you believed you were in danger, you were going to get hit and you shot him?"

"Yes."

"What did he look like?"

"When I shot him?"

"Yeah."

"Surprised. His forehead sort of lifted up like a flap and he went over backwards."

"Was there much blood?"

"Surprisingly little."

"Well, that's self-defense, Harrow. Tell the police that."

"I can't."

"Why not?"

"Because they won't believe it. They'd love to nail a lawyer like me."

"Who would?"

"The police."

"Why?"

"Because I make more money than they do."

I shook that off. "Harrow, that's stupid. You're turning an act of self-defense into murder. You chop up the body, that's what a guilty man would do." Then something crossed my mind.

"Did you give him any China White?"

"He had his own."

"Stop lying. Did you give him some?"

"A bit. At his mother's house." He paused. "Then we did a bit more here."

"Do you still have some left?"

"Yes, why?"

"Because it's evidence. You can show that to the police, it's proof that he was stoned."

"They'll never believe me."

"Why not?"

"They just won't."

"They just will, Harrow."

He looked crestfallen.

"I flushed it away."

"You did what?"

"It was evidence."

"It was evidence *for* you, Harrow, not against you. Now how are you going to prove he was stoned?"

"The autopsy."

"What if it doesn't show up in his blood?"

He considered that for a moment; I could see him give up.

"No one knows he's here," he said feebly. "We could pull it off."

"No, we couldn't, Harrow. Besides, I don't want to. There's no statute of limitations on murder. We'd have this hanging over our heads for the rest of our lives. We could be seventy-five years old out on a rocking chair and they could come and arrest us. Call the police, Harrow. Call them."

I pushed harder.

"I'm not going to ruin the rest of my life for this piece of shit." I gestured toward the body outside.

"He really was a piece of shit too."

"I know. So call the cops."

He thought for a moment.

"It's going to look bad. The kitchen, the clothes. I should clean up a bit."

"No, don't do that. Don't do anything else. Just call the police."

"It wasn't a murder," he said after a moment.

"Then don't turn it into one. Call them."

He sat silent for a moment.

"You shouldn't be here," he said. "When they come, you shouldn't be here."

That caught me off guard.

"No," he said. He was very forceful now. Very much in control of himself. "Listen, I'm going to do it, but I'm going to do it my way. I'll give you ten minutes. Then I'll call."

"Promise?"

He looked wearied at my insistence. I went out on to the porch, got on my bike, rode down the road. I stopped on the main drag. I looked back at the house. Harrow was right. It did look like the house in *Psycho.*

Chapter Eight

There's something exhilarating about being on the fringes of a crisis, a tragedy even. To this day, it causes me some discomfort to remember the days that followed the killing of Pascal Charleville, not because of the events themselves, which were extraordinary, but because of the way I was, my solemn-faced excitement, like a kid called to fight a brush fire at the side of grown men.

When I got back to Toronto that afternoon, I had another bad chill but I couldn't face going home, and so, rather dramatically, I phoned Kalie from the outskirts of the city and told her I had something to tell her. She had company, she said. In an ominous voice I told her to get rid of them.

When I arrived at her apartment in the Greek quarter, I found her sitting in the living room alone. Pacing the floor, my teeth still chattering from the chill, I recounted the whole episode. I told it in extreme detail, chronologically. I gave nothing away, no hint of what lay ahead. When I got to the part where Harrow pulled back the sleeping bag, revealing Pascal's body, Kalie dropped her hand from her chin and paled. I remember taking a kind of satisfaction in that, I realized simultaneously that a part of me was thrilled, galvanized by being part of the story. It was like an adventure. I swore her to silence, told her to tell no one, but wondered privately if I was capable of keeping the secret myself.

I sped back across town. The phone was ringing as I came in the door. It was Warren, my drunken cousin.

"I've got some very bad news," he said in a hand-me-my-sword voice. He was excited too.

"What?" I said.

"Harrow Winncup is in jail for shooting Pascal Charleville." There was a pause.

"Shooting him?" I said.

Then the surprise came. While I paused, gathering my thoughts, choosing a posture, really, Warren went on.

"He had a knife to Mrs. Winncup's throat, he was going to kill her. . . . "

"Wait a minute," I said, "who did?"

"Pascal. Mrs. Winncup dropped by the house with a roast beef for Harrow and Pascal just happened to be there."

"Uh huh?"

"He snuck up behind her with a butcher knife and put it to her throat. Harrow blew him right off her shoulder."

"She must have been covered in blood."

"I don't know," Warren mumbled.

I woke up at four o'clock in the morning. Nothing moved in the apartment. I got up and went to the bathroom, took a pee, it required tremendous concentration, I could feel myself waking up. I hurried back to bed but it was too late. I was clearheaded, refreshed from a three-hour nap. I lay in bed thinking about Harrow. I sifted through the lies, I took this piece, I took that piece, I put them together. Harrow and Pascal bought a bag of China White and drove north to get wrecked. They got rid of me and got down to business. Pascal did something to scare Harrow; he must have, I still believed that, and Harrow shot him. Then what?

I put my hands behind my head and stared up at the ceiling. Harrow was left alone in the house by himself. Just Harrow and the smoke drifting across the study and the brains gleaming on the wall. What then? Unable to sit still, he went to work. It's early afternoon, crows caw in the fields, the grass stirs in the breeze and Harrow makes his way through the house which still smells of gunpowder. He cleans the brains off the walls, he scrapes them off with a knife, the morsels falling into his open hand, then finishes the job with a kitchen sponge, puts the sponge back in the sink after rinsing it out. The blood dyes the sink bottom red, he turns on the tap; bits of brain catch like putty in the drain. He pushes them down with his finger. Then he goes into the study, grabs Pascal, drags him out the back door, leans him against the wall, strips the body, shirt, running shoes, undoes Pascal's fly, pulls his jeans off, dumps them in the rusted drum, soaks them with barbecue fluid, lights them on fire, pulls a sleeping bag down from the clothesline and covers the body. Goes back inside. Blood streaks the floor. It congeals in the cracks between the boards; he tears up a board, then another. It's hot work, makes him sweat. Gradually, the adrenaline bite wears off, his thoughts move in another direction. He stops. Looks around, the mess, the floor, the smoke rising from the backyard drum; he is falling down a well, he knows it now, this is the wrong course. In an attempt to stop himself, to grab at the slippery sides, he phones me. It's a chaotic grasp, a flinging out of the hand to a childhood friend, someone from back there who can stop the fall.

So I turn up and point the boat back toward shore. Then I leave. And then what happened? Why would he phone his mother? For protection, like dying men on the battlefield calling for their mothers.

She comes and they call the police.

No, that's not right. That's a fantasy, a cartoon; that's not what happened.

My stomach churned; I was wide awake; my hands were sweating. I stared at the ceiling. Something monstrous formed in my imagination.

No, he called his mother first; she got there *before* me. It was her idea to call me, to get me involved; she left just before I'd arrived. It'd make a cleaner story, less coincidental.

Maybe there was more, maybe she wanted to pin it on me. And Harrow, stoned, terrified, went along with it, handed over the reins to his mother, just said sure, whatever. But there was a problem. The powder burns. Harrow had powder burns on his hands. It proved it; he was the only one who could have fired the gun. Unless they could have got me to fire it. Did he try? Did he ask me to touch it, to pick it up? For fingerprints? Near daylight I called Kalie.

"They brought me up there to pin it on me. I'm sure of it."

I could feel her measure her words.

"Have you been up all night?"

"Why?"

"Your voice gets a certain sound to it."

"Yes. Most of it anyway. I was fine but then I woke up."

"I don't think that's right. I don't think that's what happened. It sounds too organized. Too evil."

"I'm sure of it," I said, my certainty slipping away.

"I think," she said delicately, "and don't snap at me, I think that you've been close to something ugly and it's made you unhappy."

My eyes watered up. I don't know how she did it, Kalie could say the simplest things to me and they just broke my heart.

"Can I come over?" I said.

It was daylight when I parked the car in front of her house. I let myself in the front door, went up the stairs, past the little boy's bed. He lay on his back, his pyjamas open, a Batman blanket partly covering his narrow chest. A blue vein ran up his rib cage. He looked so fragile, so unprotected. I covered him up.

Kalie was down the hall. She was lying in bed, wearing a long cotton nightshirt.

"Get in," she said.

I left my jeans on. I got into bed; she smelt of toothpaste. She turned her back to me. I put my arm around her waist.

"I've got an audition," she said. "I've got to get some sleep. Jesse'll be up soon."

And so, wrapped like spoons, starlings and robins hollering in the yard, we fell asleep.

I read about the killing in the newspaper the next day. I read it at Kalie's kitchen table. The article was in the bottom corner of the page, buried in the middle of the paper.

> *Musician Harrow Winncup was arrested today for the second-degree murder of Pascal Charleville. The two men were drinking at the Winncup residence when a quarrel broke out and a firearm was discharged. Mr. Winncup has been committed to the Clarke Institute of Psychiatry for a thirty-day observation period.*

That was a shock. The Clarke was right across the street from my apartment. Its narrow eyes watched over the neighbourhood; peered directly into my kitchen window. Harrow was there.

Kalie came into the kitchen while I was reading it. I showed it to her.

"Wow," she said. "The real thing."

She went over to the cupboard, pulled down a box of tea bags, looked at the watch on her long wrist, then plucked out a tea bag and dropped it on the counter.

"You know," she said, her back to me, "I could have made love to you last night."

It must have been a couple of weeks later. It was the middle of the night. I'd been dreaming about Christmas when I was a child, coming down the stairs early in the morning, the snow piled up to the window ledges, the Christmas lights blue and green.... I woke up heavy with sadness and nostalgia. I went to the kitchen window. I looked across the street, at the dark wall of the booby hatch. I wondered what window was Harrow's. I had a feeling that he was awake, that that was what had woken me up. I could feel him trapped on a locked ward floor, his eyes open. Could feel his fright.

Suddenly, unsummoned, it came back to me, the memory of reading Sonnet 30 that feverish spring night years and years ago when I wished I could rescue him from a castle, throw up a grappling hook, shimmy over a wall, do something heroic to show him my friendship.

I got dressed and walked up through the narrow back alley. Electricity hummed in the street lamps. The moon was full. Behind a dark, wooden fence, a dog's collar rattled. He was listening, getting ready to bark. I moved on. A cat glided down a fire escape. Broken glass glittered on the cement stones by the drinking fountain.

I moved up the narrow alley. This was Chinatown: sagging houses leaned together, curtains, small windows, hideous glaring interiors. At this hour, people stirred like mice, a hurrying figure disappeared into a brightly lit house. I slipped between two brick buildings and came out on College Street. A rusted Cadillac sat in front of an all-night milk store. A middle-aged Chinese man crossed my path; he was wearing a dark, marine-green suit and white topsiders. A white-haired man spoke Greek into a telephone. I crossed over the street and looked up at the Clarke. It went up twenty floors, a big, wide-chested building with those narrow windows. A tall, leafless hedge separated it from the street. I followed the hedge to the corner and turned up a still side street that led into the student quarter. There was a park bench in the shadows and I sat down on it and looked up at those windows. They were too narrow to jump out of. I wondered why that had never occurred to me before.

There were white-barked birch and pine trees growing at the

side of the booby hatch; the grass was thick and perfect. Sap gleamed on the trunks. It was very quiet. At one point, I got up and wandered over to the foot of the wall. It was some image, let me tell you, me standing there under a full moon, looking up the side of the building, like Romeo and Juliet. A figure appeared in one of the slits. The face came close to the window; it paused uncertainly, looking into the night. Then it went away again.

A streetcar slid by on metal wheels. I heard quick footsteps on cement behind me. They disappeared up the street. A single bird twittered in a tree.

I went back and sat on the bench. My back ached. The bird's song reminded me of university, of writing an Old English exam, Harrow and I and a long-haired girl leaning against a red wall after the exam.

"If I fail, I'll kill myself," the girl said.

And then we went to lunch.

Over my head, a branch dipped suddenly in the wind, its tiny green buds, like candies, caught the light from the street lamps. They were so young, so healthy, so full of life they shined.

It got cold and I put my hands in my pockets. I stayed, I don't know why, maybe because I was waiting for something else to happen. But I stayed too long, I always do, and gradually the spell dissolved and I left for home, drained and unhappy.

I sat for a while in the dark kitchen, staring across the street, too tired to get up. The phone rang. It gave me a terrible start. I picked it up. Silence.

"Harrow," I said. "Is that you?"

I heard him laugh softly.

"I can smell the chicken cooking," he said.

There was a pause. He breathed in, long and deep. It sounded medicated.

"I told the police about the first visit. But remember, just the first."

"Jesus, Harrow."

"It slipped out."

"Harrow, watch the medication. For God's sake. Watch yourself."

"I have to go. A nurse is coming."

He rang off.

Sometime later, a few days maybe, a cop phoned me at home. Identified himself as a homicide detective. Wanted to come around and talk to me. When would it be convenient? I called up Harrow at the hospital and left a message; he called me back.

"The cops called me," I said. "We better have a chat."

Later that day, I was sitting in the foyer of my apartment; out of the corner of my eye, I saw a stocky figure come to a stop beneath the window. He stood motionless, a scarf around his neck, looking up. "Hello, neighbour," he called. It was Harrow.

He ran up the stairs two at a time, very agile for a man his size. He looked better than he did the last time I saw him, although that's not saying much. His head, though, seemed slightly larger. I brought him into the kitchen. He was nervous. We both were.

"I'm out on a lunch pass," he said.

"You're having a hell of a summer," I said.

He nodded grimly. He looked out the window at the Clarke.

"Is that what I think it is?" he asked. I nodded.

"Do you mind if we shut the curtains?"

We sat at opposite ends of the table. "You look good," I said.

He frowned. "A little puffy. It's the medication."

I felt a twinge of impatience; it surprised me.

"Medication?"

It made him defensive. His brow wrinkled. I went over to the sink and filled the kettle.

"It's just something to help me sleep," he said.

"What is it?"

"Thyroxine." He paused. "And a little Valium at night."

"They used to give Librium to Jeremy Thorpe," I said. Thorpe was a boy who'd gone mad in university. I don't know why I said that, but it was rather mean-minded, rather threatening, I think.

Harrow looked thoughtful, as if the subject of Thorpe's medication were worthy of serious consideration.

"Were they little green pills?" he asked.

"Yes. I think they were."

"They might give me the odd one of those too."

Now I understood the slightly bloated face. The downers made him retain water.

But there was something else. Something about him made me suddenly irritable. I was also aware that I was perspiring, I could smell myself, an acrid, frightened smell. But what was I afraid of? Not Harrow, not physically. Perhaps I was afraid he might see how I was feeling, that it would be written on my face. Something had changed since that episode in the dandelion field, my hog-bottom friend somersaulting in the fresh grass, that obscene praying, him slumped naked in the field. I couldn't get the image out of my mind. There had been something about his physical positioning, his way of holding himself, feminine and fever-holy. I hadn't realized how it had burnt itself into my imagination, how profound my disgust with him was, until he stepped into the kitchen.

"Could we get out of here?" he said precipitously. "I've been cooped up for ages. Let's get outside."

"Just a minute," I said and the tone surprised me. It was undisguisedly patronizing, like talking to a child stamping his feet in the hall to go to the park. I don't want to make too much of it but I don't think, ever, I'd talked to him in that voice. There was in it, I realize now, a sense of impunity, of indifference to how he responded.

"How's it going?" I asked. This was terrible, foreign territory.

"The police stuff?"

"Yes."

He pondered that for a moment.

"They're pretty good guys," he said, trying for something too sad.

"No, they're not, Harrow, They're pricks. But they're not stupid."

He seemed even more agitated.

"Listen, I've got to get outside. I need some fresh air."

I wondered if he thought someone might overhear him, or maybe, it occurred to me suddenly, that I was miked.

Like strangers we went outside and started along the sidewalk.

"I'm not tape recording this, Harrow," I said.

"I know," he replied sadly. "It's just these pills. They make you jumpy. Fat and jumpy. Nice combination."

"Stop taking them."

"I can't sleep without them."

I didn't respond.

"God forbid I should have any trouble sleeping," he added with a hollow laugh and a glimpse of the old Harrow peeped out. He could still do it, pull the rug out from under himself, and win you back, just when you'd given up on him. It was as if he suddenly turned to you and said, listen, I hear this shit, I know what I'm saying, I know how fucked up it is, but what would you do in my place?

We passed the Chinese community hall.

"Did you get my letter?"

"No," I said.

"I must have got the address wrong. I was a bit socked."

We turned down Spadina Avenue. Chinatown bustled with shoppers.

"I never liked this street," he said. "It's too wide."

"Harrow," I burst in, "what the hell happened? What is this bullshit with your mother? I thought we'd come to an agreement."

"It wouldn't work," he said succinctly. "You've got to trust me on this one."

"It's crazy."

"It isn't."

"It is too."

"You don't understand. Look, I don't want to fight about this, all right? I'm fought out. There's other stuff at stake now."

We fell into a confused silence.

"So are you going to tell the police what happened?" he asked. Something stirred in me when he said that. It was heartbreaking, the simplicity, like listening to a child who has resigned himself to no Christmas.

"No, of course not."

"I don't want to go to jail," he said.

"Tell them the truth."

"I can't. It's too late."

It was too.

"What are *you* so pissed off about?" he asked.

"I'm pissed off that you're back with your mother." It came out sounding trite and petty. I waited until the antagonism left my voice.

"Is there anything I can do, Harrow? What can I do?" Something changed in him when I said it, his rhythm, the way he held himself. He looked suddenly prepared, rehearsed, as if he'd been waiting for this, no, not waiting, but rather had been trying to find a way in when, abruptly, I had thrown him a pitch right across the plate.

"Tell them you were there. You saw it happen. Ran away. Didn't want to get involved. Something like that."

He must have seen something on my face because it made him turn away, embarrassed or ashamed by the incredulity, the impossible astonishment, he saw there.

"I can't do that, Harrow."

We walked for a while in silence. I wondered if his mother put him up to it.

"So what's the booby hatch like?" I asked.

"Like university," he said.

"Are you sure you can't do this?" he asked.

"Harrow, I'm sure."

"Why?"

"Because I don't want to be involved in a lifetime project with your mother."

"I wish you'd drop that. Just for now."

"I can't."

We went into a cool, jazzy restaurant. Light pine tables and chairs, plants everywhere, rich people having brunch, a fine-boned, effeminate man sipped coffee at the bar.

"Order me something, will you?" he said. "I'm on bail. I can't drink. A Bloody Mary." I remembered the red stain on my shirt on the plane to Jamaica. Harrow went downstairs to the bathroom while I ordered. When he came back to the table, I said about the drink:

"Is this going to be all right?"

"They've got me on so many drugs at the Clarke the booze'll never show up." He looked at the tall, cold, red drink in front of him. Just the notion of it being there made him more confident.

I reached my hand over the table and touched his arm.

"Harrow, " I said. "You've got to take care of this. You can't let other people look after this for you."

"Do you know how much the lawyer costs?" he said. "A hundred grand up front. They never give you any change back. Once you write the cheque, they find a way to spend it."

"Didn't Jerry Lee Lewis shoot his bass guitarist?" I asked.

"Really?" Harrow said.

"With a .357 Magnum."

"Big gun," Harrow said. "And he got off?"

"Yep."

He fell into a preoccupied silence.

"What?" I said.

"I should have chopped him up."

"No."

"Yes," he said emphatically. It sounded almost as if he were blaming me, as if I'd got him in trouble.

"Harrow, you would have got really fucked if you'd got caught on that one."

He leaned forward, an incredulous smile animating his face.

"Whereas, as it is, things worked out just fine."

When the laughter subsided, I tried for the waiter's eye but I think he'd overheard something and he stayed away.

"No one would have known," Harrow said. "No one."

This was taking us nowhere.

"What are you going to do?" I asked.

"I might take a little trip," he said.

"Where?"

"Rio. I hear Rio's my kind of a town."

I didn't ask, but he understood what I was thinking.

"They didn't take my passport. They only do that if you're Italian. They're the only ones who fuck off."

"That's odd."

"Yeah, everyone else stays." He thought for a moment. "Problem is, I don't speak a fucking word of Spanish."

"Portuguese, I think it is."

"They speak Portuguese there? That makes no sense whatsoever."

He got up and went to the bathroom. I ordered him another drink. It arrived and I set it in front of me. A jazzy alto sax flitted among the hibiscus and rubber plants. I smelt strong, dark coffee.

Harrow came back and sat down heavily.

"Are you sure there's no way you could do this? We could help you out."

A delicate quizzicality infected his eyes.

I confess. I felt a thrill of excitement. I saw a beach in Thailand, I saw a black sound system, I saw a present for Jesse that would literally knock him to the floor with surprise. I imagined paying Kalie's rent for a month, maybe two. I could quit teaching, write a novel.

"No. No," I said. I hoped he would try harder. Find a way to make it do-able. "I don't have a moral position on this, Harrow. I didn't like Pascal. He was a bad dog that needed shooting."

"I'm in a real bind here," he said. "The brains are on the wrong wall. I moved the fucking chair. The police know it."

"Harrow, there's no statute of limitations on murder."

"I know, I know," he said.

In a while: "It's too bad you never got to know each other," he said. "You and my mother."

"Yes, well," I said. "It's too late now." We fell into a silence.

"Tell me," I whispered, "why did you shoot him?"

A wall came down between us. It wasn't me he was speaking to. It was the police.

"Because he was trying to kill my mother."

I ignored that.

"Why didn't you shoot him in the leg?"

"He had a knife to my mother's throat."

"You mustn't practise on me," I said softly.

"I'm fighting for my life here," he said.

After a while, I said, "Why the head? Why didn't you shoot him in the leg, the chest? The head, that's a tough shot."

He didn't answer.

"Harrow, that was one hell of a spectacle you put on out in that field."

"Really?"

"Really."

"I was pretty stoned."

Now wasn't the time. I let it go. The effeminate man settled his coffee cup gently on to the saucer, as if afraid to make noise. I wondered if he was listening. If he could hear.

"When's the preliminary?"

"You can't come," he said. "You're not invited."

"Maybe you should invite Tom Murphy," I said. "He could do the honours."

Harrow shook his head wearily and stared out the window. A pause.

"I should have chopped him up," he said.

Chapter Nine

When I came home the following Monday there were two cops standing in the foyer of the apartment building: a heavy-set, weary man and a pencil-thin, red-haired Scot. Detective Ray Gomes and his partner. I didn't get the name. They followed me upstairs. Gomes was breathing heavily. He was in bad shape. He sat down and looked around the apartment. I offered them coffee which they politely refused. The red-haired man said nothing.

"Look," Gomes began. "We don't care about the drugs or nothing. That's not what we're after. We thought maybe you could help us clear up some of the confusion about what went on that day."

He paused, opened his briefcase, brought out a clean pad of paper and took out a ball-point.

"Nice neighbourhood," he said.

"Do you know it?"

"I worked out of 52 Division when I was starting out. You know where that is?"

"Yes."

"What kind of relationship does Harrow have with his mother?"

Boy, that didn't take long. They were right on the buzzer, those guys. I wondered if Harrow knew how smart they were.

"I don't know," I said.

"What kind of a relationship do you have with her?"

I wanted to tell them she was a cunt. But I knew I'd be sorry.

"We hardly know each other."

"That's not the impression we got from her."

"What impression did you get from her?"

"That there was a little friction."

"No friction. That was a long, long time ago."

Gomes appeared not to have heard.

"Did you help Harrow clean up?"

"No. I wasn't even there."

He looked at his notepad. I jumped in before he could correct me. "I mean I was there early on, before the stuff happened."

"What do you do for a living? You're a teacher? Well, not quite a teacher." He looked at his notes. He held them toward the light. At arm's length. It gave him a vulnerable, even disorganized air. Where were his glasses? Why didn't he wear them?

"What's your point?"

"My point is we were hoping you could help us clear up this mess."

"I told you I wasn't there."

"Did the Winncups pay you to say that?"

"No."

"We could get your bank records." Gomes sighed wearily and again looked around the apartment. He was right. It did look like the apartment of someone who needed money; somebody bribable.

"Mr. Blackwood," he said, "we think you were there. We think that you had nothing to do with the killing. But you were there. You may have helped clean up, I'm not sure. But you're in very serious trouble and I think you need some help. And the Winncups are not going to do it for you. Not from the impression I got from Mrs. Winncup."

"Well, I wasn't there."

"You're sure?"

"Of course I'm sure."

"There's something not right here."

They stood up. Gomes shrugged.

Then they left.

That afternoon it rained like a son of a bitch. Drops clung to the windowpanes. Water overran the sewers. Cars had their headlights on. I talked to Jesse on the phone; he had a small cough; it kept him home from school. Then it got dark, rain gleamed off the streets. I was antsy and depressed. Things irritated me. The television downstairs came up through the floor. I stomped a couple of times. Nothing happened.

Around eight o'clock, there was a knock at the door. Two uniformed police officers huddled under the eaves.

"I was just watching television," I said.

The larger of the two laughed unpleasantly. "You're not watching anything," he said.

They drove me downtown. I was curiously chatty; from the way they responded, I could tell they were used to it, it was the way frightened people behaved. They sat me in a drab green room and then left. There was a table, an ashtray and two empty chairs. Graffiti on the wall. I got up to read it when the door opened and in came Detective Gomes and his silent partner, who glared at me with extraordinary menace.

"No way you weren't there," Gomes said. He took a breath, held it for a second and soundlessly shifted gears. "You don't have a record or nothing, we checked that." A pause. A look of mild but theatrical perplexity.

"I'll tell you, Christian, you're a bright guy. I'm just not sure how long you'd survive in an eight-by-ten cell."

"Meaning what?"

"There's something screwy about you, mister," the small Scot said. His eyes gleamed with malice as if, given a moment's privacy, he'd beat me unconscious with those small fine-boned fists.

Gomes frowned.

"I don't understand the unpleasantness," I said. There was a whine to my voice, a plangent tone that they must have heard. It was the whine of the guilty, the deal-maker, the about-to-crumble. The about-to-weep.

"This is a murder, Christian. It's their first murder. We do it all the time. You don't want to throw your lot in with those guys. They're amateurs."

Gomes took a thoughtful, deep sigh and stared at the ceiling. He pursed his moist lips as though calculating and then returned his gaze to me.

"I'm reasonable. My partner's reasonable. At least most days." The Scot smiled. I relaxed. I couldn't help myself, I was grateful. "So I'll tell you what I'm going to do. I want you to come back here within twenty-four hours and tell me exactly what happened." He paused. Then continued softly and carefully. "Or I'm going to come and arrest you at eight o'clock tomorrow night. And I'm going to charge you with second-degree murder. And you and your lawyer friend, Harrow, are going to go to jail, hand in hand."

He waited for it to sink in.

"Now, off you go."

I went home that night; I didn't sleep. I sprang out of bed at four o'clock in the morning, determined to call the police, to get it over with. But I hesitated. I couldn't stand the idea of having been so successfully bullied; like a small-time crook, a car thief, a cheque bouncer, shitting in my pants, rolling over on anyone who's there. I sure as hell wasn't going to the cross for the sake of Harrow Winncup, but I didn't want him to go to jail either. Well, maybe for a while but not for twenty-five years–that was the mandatory sentence–not for a scumball like Pascal Charleville. I stared at the tiles on the kitchen floor. I made a deal with myself; cowardly, but a deal. I'd wait until eight o'clock tomorrow night. I'd wait until they came and just before they arrested me, just before they charged me, I'd tell them what they wanted to know. It wasn't heroic but it was better than a middle-of-the-night snitch.

I turned on the television; around daybreak I went for a walk. Then I slept until noon. The day passed agonizingly slowly. Around six o'clock I went and packed a little overnight bag. At 7:45 there was a knock on the door. I went downstairs. I felt sick with dread. I opened the door. It was Kalie.

"I was just in the neighbourhood," she said brightly. Then, seeing my face, she said, "Are you with someone?"

We went back upstairs. I sat on the floor. I couldn't get comfortable. My legs twinged. I kept having to get up and give them a shake. Then it was five-to-eight. I almost held my breath. I looked at the clock. I looked at the television. The show changed. My hands were damp. I could smell myself. I got up and paced back and forth. I sat down beside Kalie. I had a terrible taste in my mouth. It was like blood. I was afraid to breathe on her. Then it was five past eight and then quarter past. They never came.

Sometime later, maybe a week, I ran into Claire Powers in a bar. He was the artistic director of the Front Porch Theatre. He was a manic talker, a chain smoker, an alcoholic, a bullshitter, the kind of guy who made you wonder why he hadn't been punched to death in grade school. He had a revolting habit of picking his teeth with a toothpick and then sniffing the end.

But I was lonely, I wanted company, so I sat down beside him at the bar and had a stiff one. I meant not to, but he kind of seduced me, and I told him about Harrow. The whole fucking story.

"You should write a play about it," he said. "You're just the man."

Now Claire was always saying that kind of stuff, getting drunk in bars and offering actors parts and directors plays and then forgetting about it by the following morning. He'd disappointed a lot of people; he just couldn't resist the temptation to show off, to act the brilliant, mercurial, unpredictable genius. In fact, he was an asshole with a hell of a drinking problem and normally I wouldn't have given him five minutes but that night I would have had a drink with the devil if they'd wheeled him out.

After the bar closed I went back to the theatre with him; we drank a bottle of red wine, then we went to an after-hours bar in Kensington Market. It was a damp, dark place, but I liked it. It reminded me of the Cavern in Liverpool. I saw a beautiful girl with hennaed hair and I started to tell her about the murder. I couldn't shut up, but it wasn't her kind of a story or maybe she thought I was lying, coming on to her with a piece of made-up bullshit. She cut me off politely and suddenly I was looking at her back. I sat down on a ratty sofa and listened to Claire browbeat some poor actor. He had the drop on them, they needed work, he had a theatre and I despised him for not getting that, for not understanding why actors paid him heed. It seemed like bad luck to be with a guy like that, as if I were a loser.

But I stayed. I didn't want to go home.

Things shifted. The booze moved me forward to a new square.

Suddenly, I wanted to go up and see the house where Harrow shot Pascal. It seemed very important. Claire went along with it; he wanted to be around the heat. He thought it was real life, real issues, real stakes. He must have said it a dozen times.

So Claire and I got in his car and headed north, out of town. We popped a Bob Marley tape in the machine; it gave things a cinematic flare, a kind of soundtrack for our rush through the spring night. Soon we were driving along a dark country road. A bright moon hung in the sky. On the horizon, a bright light glowed in the yard of a farmhouse. We passed the house where I saw the kid in the hammock. Claire pulled the car to the side of the road and slid his lean, chain-smoking, overexcited frame out of the seat. I got out and we stood at the side of the road. The air smelt clean and wonderful. What a waste, I thought, this beautiful countryside, the air, the moon in a clear sky and Harrow with nothing better to do than get wrecked. Then I started along the dark road. Claire walked behind me. I could hear the scuffle of stones. We arrived in front of the house. It sat like a black smudge, just off the road. The barn soared up behind it. A star twinkled in the sky, then another and another and another. And then I saw the sharp, shocking image of Harrow rolling naked in the dandelion field.

I looked at the house. I waited to feel something, some terror, some sense of evil, but nothing came. It was like being in a room with a corpse.

"The vibes are intolerable," Claire said, holding his head and backing away. "It's like the walls of the house are dripping blood!"

If you believe in the big leagues, you should never spend time with a guy like Claire.

"I'm telling you," he whispered breathlessly, "you should write a play about this guy. It's a natural."

It was summer, exploding, shimmering, sap-running, sun-sweating summer. It seemed to have happened overnight. Lilac blossoms stirred in the soft wind. A girl in a sleeveless T-shirt bicycled under my window. I watched the postman move down the street, disappearing up a shaded lane, then back out again into the hot, bright sunlight. When I heard the clank of my mail chute, I put down the newspaper and went downstairs to see if there was anything for me. There was a phone bill, a cheque from the Board of Education, a handbill for a new neighbourhood Chinese restaurant, a fundraising announcement from my old school, an advertisement for a new show at the Front Porch Theatre. Claire Powers must have put me on the mailing list. I took the letters back upstairs and opened up the cheque. It was for more than I'd expected. I'd buy a toaster, I thought, or a new printer ribbon; maybe both.

It was the summer holidays.

Kalie got a job playing Masha in *Three Sisters* at the Edmonton Citadel.

I ran into my cousin Warren one afternoon. He showed me a photograph that had been taken the week before, up north at the Winncup house on Nine Mile Lake. It was a picture of a red-faced, unshaven Harrow with a chainsaw hanging like a weapon from his belt. It was supposed to be funny, to be tough, but it left a bad taste in my mouth. I'm just not sure you ought to be posing for shots like that if you just killed somebody.

"He's living across town," he said. "You should give him a call."

I got a drunken phone call from Claire.

"You should write that play, you know. The Harrow story. Top to bottom. There's no one in Canada writing about that class, about how they end up. You should do it. I'd direct it myself." I could hear the clank of dishes and voices in the background. He was calling from a bar, performing, I guessed, for a table of actors nearby. I wouldn't have trusted him to put on a dog show.

I remember watching a lot of videos that month. It sounds bleak, but it wasn't. It was sort of like a project to see all the classics I'd missed. I found a little treasure called *Songwriter.* It made me think about Kalie, it made me very dewy-eyed, I called her up long distance but it was right after a show, she was still zipped and peremptory and I could feel the romance slip out of me like air from a rip in a balloon. I don't mean it was her fault. It was just timing, just bad luck. But God I was depressed when I put down the phone. Really flattened out.

I got a nifty contract though, that week I think, writing a series of anti-smoking brochures for the Ministry of Health. It was a good score, dull, but it meant a steady income all summer and, shallow as it may sound, that made me happy. Until I got used to it anyway.

About what happened next. I'd like to say it was the result of a fresh wound, that Harrow provoked it. But I know now that's not true, that I would have done it anyway.

I'm trying to figure out, to this day, why I did what I did. Could I really have been that vengeful, that full of childhood hatred? I can now see a string, no, a chain, linking a series of apparently random events. It may be the only long-term plan I've ever carried out. I'd never have believed myself capable of such method, such focus and patience. Not to mention a kind of self-deception that, in another, I would describe as mental illness. But who knows? Maybe that's just how I look at it this year, a creative turn on events to prevent me from growing bored with them. But on the other hand, it occurred to me last night that maybe Florence Winncup was right about me when I was a kid, that I was dangerous, someone to watch out for. I mean I didn't just give them a kick in the shins, I shoved a garden rake up their ass and then yanked it out, hard. But I'm getting ahead of myself.

The preliminary took place during the first week of June, the purpose being for the court to decide if there was enough hard evidence to go to trial on a second-degree murder charge.

The courthouse was a big white square building in the middle of a field a half hour's drive north of the city. It was supposed to be a tough district, tough judges, long waits, but I don't know. Harrow got in fast enough.

I got there at nine in the morning. Florence was seated on a wooden bench outside courtroom nine. She looked frumpy, deliberately plain, a shapeless white dress, a modest scarf around her neck, her hair up in a bun; a simple gold wedding-band on her finger; that hunk of green emerald was gone. It's curious. I felt a sort of shock when I saw her, as if I should duck, not be seen. But then I caught myself. I went right over. I put out my hand.

"Hello Florence."

This time, though, she responded with relief, almost affection, not for me, but for my familiarity, like running into an acquaintance in a foreign country. It was hard to resist it. I've always found it hard to resist people who are kind to me. I shook hands with her daughter. Dorian looked lovely and fragile, she puffed on a cigarette and blew the smoke away from me.

"It's good to see you again, Christian," she said with that odd formality. The sunlight poured in the window and in the natural light she looked very pale but very desirable. There's something about early mornings in an institution that catches you right in the groin. Across the hall a lawyer leaned against a wall, a coffee cup in his hand, and talked to a black man. He was a smug young pup, this attorney, with a head full of quick, condemning opinions.

I watched him for a second. Two police officers walked by me.

Then Harrow appeared. He was too closely shaved, it made his face shine. Wearing a grey cashmere suit, he made his way slowly down the middle of the crowded hallway, flanked by two fat attorneys. Fatty 1, the big gun, had a red alcoholic face, a deep voice, a craggy profile, like a decadent Roman senator. Florence and her daughter rose. There were cheerful greetings, smiles all around, it was very friendly; for that money, it ought to be.

A few moments later I saw Zinta Strom hurry along the hall. She looked surprisingly old. A lot of time must have passed. I hadn't realized it. Someone told me she'd had a minor stroke a year or two before. I recalled this because just as she joined us, she butted out a long white cigarette in a stand-up ashtray. She seemed surprised to see me. Mrs. Winncup engaged her in a short conversation. Zinta paid hard attention. She was still at it, still hoping the gate would open and they'd let her into the family. Maybe this was it, this was a chance to perform beautifully in a crisis. I stood off to the side and watched Zinta talk. It seemed so odd now, such a peculiar activity, that I had kissed her lips, her neck, her shoulders. So remote.

The traffic, the humanity rushed by me. It was eerily festive. Police and lawyers and crooks and child-support evaders and break-and-enter guys, squirrels with bad skin in heavy-metal T-shirts, a plump black woman done up to the nines and her perfectly neat kids, all chatting together while the cars pulled in and out of the parking lot outside.

In a little while Warren came along; he was all scrubbed, like a poor boy going to Sunday school, his hair still wet, an ill-fitting shirt hung around his neck. He was excited, you could tell, he just couldn't wait to get inside the court.

I glimpsed a face as it disappeared into the courtroom. It looked at me quickly then looked away. It was Tom Murphy, the little prick who went to Jamaica with Harrow all those years ago.

Harrow came over by himself. We shook hands rather formally. He looked hung over.

"Nice suit," I said.

"Jumbo size," he answered.

Then a bell rang and we all went into the courtroom.

It was exciting at first, just being there, the institutional authority of the proceedings. A man with a bald pate and Bozo the Clown hair got up and began to speak. He was a lie-detector expert, he loved the spotlight, he adjusted his cuffs while he spoke, he went into extreme and self-congratulatory detail; he fancied himself a very interesting chap indeed. He must have talked for forty-five minutes; he talked about the history of lie detection, the early instruments, the arguments pro and con. He went on and on and I almost missed his point when he made it: Florence Winncup had passed a lie-detector test.

Now that was a wake-up call. These people could even fool machines. I almost laughed out loud but then I realized I wanted to be seen laughing, to inspire doubt; a part of me, evidently, didn't want Harrow to get away with this. And I was aware, ever so slightly, that a depression had settled over me like a fine coating of dust. I was in a funk because the lie-detector man had made such a strong, favourable impression on the judge. It's not that I wanted Harrow found guilty and hanged. I just didn't want these Winncups to get away scot-free with such a nonsensical alibi.

Then a forensic expert got up, a man with a peanut head, horn-rimmed glasses and a hesitant manner. He was a sad sight; his clothes didn't have the snap, the vitality of the clown man. He described a laboratory test where he'd fired Harrow's shotgun, one blast at point-blank range into the side of a pig's head. The results? Well, he said, if Harrow were standing behind the desk, as he said he was, then Pascal's brains would have been on a different portion of the wall. It was said in a very matter-of-fact manner, nothing personal; he wasn't enjoying himself, in fact he appeared to find public speaking distasteful. It made him credible and dangerous. Everyone was freshly impressed. I looked at Harrow. He and his mother gave each other stern nods, the nods of the grim innocent.

It appeared to be a draw.

But then a detective produced a small tape recorder and turned it on. We heard Harrow's voice. It was a slow, twelve-bar blues.

If you want to be a fool
You can always go to school

If you want to be a suck
Then you'll have to learn to duck

So get yourself a hobby
Do it in your home
Buy yourself a pistol
And you'll never be alone.

So buy a gun
Buy a gun
And have yourself some fun.

They played the whole thing, five verses and a hook. Mrs. Winncup looked confused, as if she didn't recognize the voice. Quite a performance, right out of *Masterpiece Theatre.*

Harrow whispered something to his lawyer, who stood up and addressed the judge.

"Your honour, my client did not write the lyrics for that song." The judge stopped writing and looked up. "He didn't write the song?" he asked with mild surprise.

"Mr. Winncup wrote the melody but not the lyrics."

"Who wrote the lyrics?"

"Someone else."

"I need a name, counsellor."

The lawyer took off his glasses. "I don't know, your honour."

"Did *you* write them, counsellor?"

The lawyer smiled deferentially.

"No, your honour."

He conferred with Harrow, scribbled something on a sheet of paper, then rose to his feet.

"A Mr. Christian Blackwood wrote the words, I believe." He consulted the paper again, myopically, to confirm the name. The judge paused.

"Is this germane, counsellor?"

"Given the nature of the lyrics, your honour, we think so."

"Taken under consideration," the judge said and resumed his writing.

Suddenly I heard a voice hiss in my ear. It came from right behind me.

"This is the biggest audience you'll ever get for anything."

It was Tom Murphy. Blue pin-striped suit, tennis tan, expensive haircut. I could smell a vigorous after-shave. I opened my mouth to reply, I confess nothing came immediately, when a security guard scowled at me and pointed threateningly to the door. I shut my mouth; Tom sat back with evident satisfaction. It was a clean hit, no retaliation.

The detective touched a small button on the tape recorder. The song started up again.

If your baby comes home late
Tells you she's had enough
Ain't no good to slap her
Or even treat her rough.

I say bullets to the left
Bullets to the right.
Keep on talkin' baby
'Cause I got you in my sights.

The courtroom was silent; everyone watched the small, motionless black machine. Very slowly, as if on a timer, Florence Winncup's head turned and looked at me. I meant to hold her glance, but I couldn't. For the first time since I was a child I felt a shred of compassion for her.

They broke for lunch just before noon. The doors opened and we spilt into the corridor in a cluster. Zinta lit a cigarette. So did Dorian. They shared a little joke, about smoking in court. Zinta cupped a hand over her eyes in my direction. I had the distinct sense of being on the outside of things, as usual, but it felt different now, I sort of liked it, it sort of distinguished me, although, I admit, it was as if I had to continually remind my body, my nervous system, that things had changed, that I was no longer a child lingering in the radius of an unfriendly adult. There was, no question about it, a part of my memory, a part of who I was, which seemed unaffected, untouched, by anything that had happened since Forest Hill. The new stuff seemed to have gone into a pocket *beside* it, which, though bigger, was never where I reached when I reached instinctively. In fact, I needed reminding it was there, that it was the more important of the two. More current anyway. I wondered also, quickly, incongruously, if my life was over, if I was getting ready to die. Because that first pocket, it seemed more often these days that that's where my real life, my *receptiveness* to life, lay. But it was shut now, sewn up, healed; nothing went in there any more.

Harrow broke away from the group and walked over. "I'll tell you," he whispered, "that was some kind of weird when they played that song. Wow!"

Then he wrinkled his brow and said, "I've got to have lunch with my lawyers." I don't think he wanted me to feel ignored, it was a damn strange thing for a man on trial for murder to be worried about. But very Harrow. Tom Murphy, I couldn't help noticing, dithered at the end of the hall. I think he was waiting for Harrow. I had the small, petty but insistent thought, why would *he* be invited to lunch with Harrow's lawyers and not me? Was I still the unpresentable one? I was getting a little tired of this.

I didn't want to get trapped at a table making small talk with Warren, I didn't want to be perceived to be on that team, seated at the loser's table, so I wandered around in the parking lot while everyone got settled in the cafeteria. I ate a sandwich on the stone steps. I pulled out a paperback, but it made me sleepy so I put it away and went outside for a walk. For a second there it was as if I were supply-teaching again, it was the same kind of exhaustion.

When court resumed I took my place on the bench at the back of the court. It didn't take long though. Sometime after two the judge decided there was enough evidence to proceed to trial on a murder charge and he adjourned the court. Zinta lit up again, held her cigarette at her side, her hand stiff and slightly turned out. I pretended to buy a newspaper from a recalcitrant box. The group moved to the end of the hall.

"Come with us," Harrow said to me, as though coaching a shy sophomore from his residence room.

We went across the parking lot to a gaudy steak house, Harrow,

Florence, Dorian, Warren, and Zinta. Tom Murphy had slipped away. We sat at a circular table. I went to the bathroom to make sure I looked all right, that I didn't have newsprint smudged on my face or something awful in the corner of my eye. When I came back, Florence was talking about Gorbachev.

"I don't care, I think he's the anti-Christ. And who was that appalling woman?" she inquired with sudden irritation. "The woman in the dress with the cows on it?"

Warren laughed.

"What is that thing on her back? Why is she hunched over like that?"

"It's a growth," Harrow said absently.

"She looks like Richard III," Florence said.

A swarthy waiter came over.

We ordered a round of drinks.

"You should see how they do things in Russia, Dorian," she said. "You wouldn't always take their side." Very prettily, Dorian exhaled a lungful of smoke and batted it away from her face and then laughed pointlessly.

The conversation stuttered. Everyone wanted the drinks to come.

"He's so ... Slavic," said Zinta, and again she gave Harrow a meaningful look. Warren laughed again. He was having a vivid, exciting time. He was sitting at the grown-up table.

"How did you get here, Christian?" Dorian asked. Her mother watched me impassively. They still needed me, she knew it, so she kept herself in check.

"By motorcycle," I said.

Harrow pursed his lips. He was thinking about Jamaica, about that long smooth ride down Bamboo Avenue, the sun roasting our backs, the wind blowing over the cane fields, down, down we went, before the hill pulled up and took off into the blue mountains. "I'm selling the Callington place," Harrow said to me.

"Makes sense," I said.

"It was always a compromise. I'm moving to the Danforth."

"Why *that* part of town?" Zinta asked, frowning, as if the

question were serious or important.

"We're taking a trip first," Florence said.

"I want to go back to Ethiopia," Harrow said. "It's a holy place."

I didn't like hearing the word *holy* from Harrow's lips. It brought back a bad memory.

"You should come," he said to me. Why did he say things like that? When would I go? Before the trial? After the trial? Twenty-five years from now?

The drinks arrived. Mrs. Winncup slipped a Tom Collins in front of Harrow.

At the next table, a small-faced man in a suit assured his client, "If you go for the assault, I can have you out and walking around in nine months."

Dorian caught my eye. "How've you been?" she mouthed.

I nodded. "Good," I said. She knew too. I could tell.

"Harrow, did we turn the car lights off? The headlights?" Mrs. Winncup spoke with exaggerated thoughtfulness, on purpose, I think, to let Dorian and I speak undisturbed. What's she up to? I wondered.

"Did we turn the car lights off? The headlights?"

Warren, feeling the effect of his first drink, ventured a joke.

"Jumper cables is something they'll have up *here*, believe me."

There aren't many people who would make a joke about the electric chair with a man just going into a murder trial, but Warren did. And Harrow laughed and shook his head with admiration or affection or irony, I couldn't tell.

"My kids like to get up close," Zinta said to Dorian. Zinta was a school teacher. "They can smell it on you," she went on. Smell what? Cigarette smoke? Booze? Murder?

"Who was that ... person?" Dorian asked, knowing full well the answer.

"The crown," Harrow said.

"He was a real shit."

"Dorian," her mother censured.

Harrow's lawyer joined us, a big-eyed man in a brown suit.

"How did it go?"

"They didn't lay a glove on us," he said.

"And the judge," Harrow asked with polite professionalism, "what did you make of him?"

"Defense-oriented. Understands the meaning of reasonable doubt. Can't ask for much more."

"I thought he was a shit too," Dorian said. The attorney ordered a steak sandwich with French fries. "Goodness, you remind me of your mother," Florence said to me. "She had the same way of sitting. Like that, with her hands folded."

I nodded.

"Some days I think I must call Virginia and tell her a little bit of news. I almost reach for the phone." It occurred to me suddenly that they had been very involved with each other, these two women; that my mother had loved her, had ached when she'd been dropped.

"But she loved Mexico, didn't she?" Florence said.

"It was very good to her," I said neutrally. I put my drink down. It was making me muddy; shoots of hostility stirred in moist earth.

"She was a great woman," Dorian said, propped up in her chair like a mannequin, eyes wide as saucers with tranquilizers.

A television played on the bar. A waiter watched it.

"We have a neighbour like that," Florence said.

"Right next door to us," Dorian added.

"It's like an assault."

"They don't watch it, they just need it on."

"For company."

"Where do you live?" Mrs. Winncup asked me.

"In Chinatown," I began, but she lost interest. The neighbour's television blazed up in her imagination like a field of cicadas at nightfall.

We were interrupted by the arrival of a tweedy, grey man worn thin by drink. In his shiny-assed corduroy suit, he seemed like a gentle soul, weak but *simpatico.* I couldn't figure out what his connection was. Something else. I vaguely recognized his name.

It was Jerry something, but I couldn't place it. Florence gave him a perfunctory smile. Plainly, he was early and she didn't like it.

"The furnace man came," Jerry said. "He says we need it cleaned."

There was a strange jolt in the air, like expensive material ripping on a nail. I couldn't figure out what it was. I looked at her finger. There was no wedding band on it. She wasn't married. Then I got it. She must live with him, I thought, but she doesn't want anyone to know it. It was the same kind of logic, of social paranoia, that had driven her to make Harrow flush his dope down the toilet. With a dead body on the floor, they'd been worried about a drug scandal, a blemish on Harrow's reputation.

"All right, Jerry," she said coldly.

"Hi, Jerry," said Harrow, coming gently to his defense. Jerry flushed with pleasure.

"He said it hadn't been cleaned in five years," he explained to Harrow.

"Where do I know that name from?" I asked.

"Hey, Jerry," Warren said, "Do you know 'That's Amore'? Christ, I love that song!"

Then I remembered: twenty years before, Jerry Hopper had written the theme song for Toronto's birthday. It was a catchy little tune; it even made the charts for a while.

The attorney's food arrived. He bent his red face over a smoking pile of mashed potatoes and meat and forked in a mouthful.

"Strange thing about the weather," popped in Zinta. "One minute it's cloudy, the next minute it's sunny."

"It's the ozone," said Warren.

Florence glared wrathfully at the television on the bar.

"For God's sake!" she said. She raised her arm to call over the waiter.

Harrow was staring at me, his face pale and utterly immobile.

Chapter Ten

Some weeks later, I was in my kitchen, trying to retrieve an envelope from behind the fridge when suddenly I remembered it was Harrow's birthday. I hadn't heard from him since the preliminary and I thought a call might cheer him up. It was early evening. I called him at his apartment and invited him downtown for a drink.

"Sure," he said. "That'd be lovely." But he sounded guarded. "I can't stay too long. I've got to drive up to Callington. A water main broke somewhere between the well and the house and I've got to turn it off."

"Let's have a few quick ones and off you go."

I hurried out to a bookstore and bought him a new biography of Tolstoy. I wanted to read it myself. I met him around seven. It was the dinner hour. The bar was warm and friendly. We spent an hour together, we touched on the trial, the attorney. He was cautious, but that was understandable. He didn't want to make a mistake. It was after all a twenty-five-year fall, with ten before parole.

After a while, he said he had to go. He got up, a bit drunk, I gave him a hug, and he took off. Minutes later I looked down and saw that he'd left the present behind. I ran out to the street but he was gone. I knew he was planning to stop off at his mother's first so I jumped in a cab.

It was summer now, still light out, but the cars had their headlights on and the street lamps shone with bright theatricality against the pale sky.

The cab went straight up Yonge Street, turned left on to St. Clair, pulled past Fran's restaurant, past the Granite Towers.

"Used to be the old Granite Club," the driver said.

"I know."

"They never let Jews in there. Not at first. Not till they made them."

That surprised me. My parents belonging to an anti-Semitic club?

"Are you sure?"

"Sure I'm sure. My uncle was a charter member."

A cold black office tower rose up. A pretty girl drove by in a blue car.

We passed a drab two-storey building. It used to be a discotheque. I took a girl there once in high school. She was with me, then a couple of years later she was with Harrow. I couldn't go anywhere in this city without running into small, ineradicable monuments to our having grown up together. Up north in Forest Hill, all the way down to the lake front, Harrow and I had saturated these streets with episodes and love affairs and break-ups and drugged walks and disappointed monologues and bright, insouciant look-at-us Saturday afternoons.

A tire screeched, a car pulled quickly out into the traffic and hurried away. A woman, so pale it seemed half her blood was gone, walked by in a black coat. It was neither day nor night, it sat between the two. The trees were bare and cinematic against that sky.

We turned up Dunvegan Road. We went up a hill and down the other side and a few blocks later the cab pulled to a stop in front of the Winncups' grey stone house. A television glowed high up in a corner room. I rang the front doorbell. I waited a few moments but no one answered. I stepped around the side of the house and peeked through a pair of low, leaded windows. A party raged inside. Half my friends from Upper Canada were there, people I hadn't seen in years. I recognized Tim Noble, Peter Barnes, Willie Stimes, Marshall Webb, Daphne Grant, Jane Roadouse, Tom Murphy. I saw Dorian, Zinta, the fat lawyer, Warren. And there was Harrow, a glass of champagne in his hand. I tried to steal away but at that very moment the door opened.

Florence Winncup's face dissolved into that terrible smile, the head tilted. "Hello," she said. A tick of impatience or displeasure sparked at the side of her mouth but she stopped it.

"Would you like to come in?"

Flabbergasted, I stepped in the door.

The smile remained fixed.

"And would you like some champagne?"

I don't know why, confusion, panic, childhood fright, but I said yes.

She brought me a glass of champagne. She did all this quickly, as something to be gotten over with.

Harrow looked over; he beamed with surprise, with discomfort, with guilt, with defensiveness, with aggression, with compassion; it was like a rock cracking a mirror and every piece bore a different emotion. He pushed his way over.

"Happy birthday!" he declared and gave a big, phony farmer's laugh.

I said nothing, I just kind of nodded and made a distorted face. I was afraid to look at him because he'd see clearly what was on my face, what I was feeling, which I loathed because it was old, old, old.

I didn't finish my drink, I put it half-finished on the mantelpiece and left while he was chatting to Tom Murphy. I waved from the door. When I got outside, the sky was a deep blue and a single star shone over the building.

I knew why he'd done it, why he'd "neglected" to mention the party. It was his fucking mother again. She'd thrown the party for him, she didn't want me there, he'd gone along with it. As usual. It was vintage Harrow. Say nothing, hope no one notices. The lie by omission, not really a lie at all. The dishonest, lying, cocksucking motherfucker. I'd had an ass full of the whole bunch, I'll tell you, and now I was going to fuck them proper. I was going to write a play, a simple little tale about the killing of Pascal Charleville.

The next day I went down to the Front Porch Theatre. I went in the front door. It smelt like sawdust inside. A sort of hippy girl with a colourless face and a sagging bosom looked up and asked me, coldly, if she could help me. A cigarette smouldered in the ashtray beside her elbow.

The next thing I remember is sitting in a littered office with Claire Powers. He was perched on the side of a chair, on its arm actually, he had so much energy he couldn't sit in it properly.

"What do you want to call it?" he asked.

I thought for a moment.

"Extreme People."

"Come on," he said, "I want to talk to you about something." He took a sniff of his toothpick and scrambled to his feet. I followed him down a flight of dusty stairs. He opened the doors and turned on the lights in the small, backspace theatre. He pointed to the empty stage. "That's where we'll put the kitchen, the study over here.... We'll hire Jamie Dingwall to do the head. We have to have an exploding head. He's the only one in the country who can do it." He looked around. "God, I feel like getting really fucking wrecked today," he said.

There was a small fridge in the corner; he pulled out a couple of beers.

"When you talk to the press ..." The words had a magic effect on me. They were supposed to. Talk to the press? Why would the press want to talk to me?

It was deliriously exciting and after two beers on an empty stomach, I caught a glimpse of my life in its new, untrammelled thrust, a series of electric moments one after the other. There would be no pause, no hesitation, just constant forward movement. No place visited twice.

Claire put his feet up on the seat. As if reading my thoughts–he'd flattered men before–he said, "It's happening. It's done."

I looked at him in mute astonishment.

"Really, it's done?"

"Yes."

"You're really going to put it on?"

"Yep."

"In here?"

"Yep."

I shook my head. "Can I have something in writing? Something just to look at occasionally?"

He sprang to his feet.

"Just a minute," he said and darted out of the theatre. I heard his footsteps on the stairs. Then they were gone and I was left alone in the empty theatre. I walked over to the window and looked out. Two boys ran down the street, the sun cut through the window on to the colourless floorboards. There was that smell again, sawdust, staleness. I opened the window. It was an old crank affair, like the kind in Harrow's bedroom in Forest Hill. I unwound it slowly and warm air blew in over my face. It smelt heavenly, like grass and trees and lilacs. It was sexy and sad and evocative and thrilling. I saw an image of myself as a child walking down Forest Hill Road, a cold stream of water running in the gutter. It must have been spring; the sun reflected off the water; it turned blinding silver and froze into my memory.

It was stone quiet in that theatre. A rope hung from a light. A chair lay overturned at the back of the stage. It seemed I had waited all my life for a day like this, perfect and poetic, when I didn't, for once, wish for something more, for a novel in a store window, a pretty girl in the back of a taxi, when there was no hesitation in the face of a beautiful day, no "if only ..." Across the street the bushes stirred in the wind.

I suddenly knew that this was as good as it was ever going to be, like being in a train that's pulling into the station: sure to arrive but not there yet. Everything still a glorious, weightless possibility. A bumblebee buzzed at the window. Reggae music poured from a passing car. Then a little boy in a blue shirt came walking along the street, his fingers tapping his thumb. He reminded me of Jesse; he passed under a tree and then without warning he leapt up, he leapt way high up, twisted his little body, his shirt rising up over his blue-veined stomach. He sailed up and touched a low hanging branch and then settled back to earth.

Then he moved on, having already forgotten the branch and the tree, his fingers tapping his thumb while he looked steadily ahead.

I heard footsteps on the stairs; running shoes on cement. The theatre door blasted open. Claire burst in holding a sheet of paper in his hand. "Here," he said. "Look at this." He handed it to me.

The letter was very simple, written in longhand on theatre stationery. "This is an agreement between Christian Blackwood and the Front Porch Theatre to undertake a mainstage production of *Extreme People* for the fall season, 1992."

"This fall?" That was *before* the trial.

He nodded vigorously, keeping his eyes on me. "Fuck 'em if they can't take a joke," he said.

When I got back downstairs I swung open the door and stepped into the heat and the noise. A man washed his car down the street. I walked half a block. I read the letter again. *I have a play on.* It was true, it was happening at last. I broke into a small trot. Blood raced up through the centre of my body. Suddenly, there were so many things I wanted to do, things I'd held off until just this moment. I wanted to read *The Great Gatsby* right now. Finally I could read it without feeling sick with envy. I wanted to look up old friends. I was curious, hungry to know how their lives had turned out. I wanted to get drunk, I wanted to go to the gym, I wanted to look up an old English teacher, the one who told me in grade twelve I was going to fail. What was his name? I made a plan to find him. I wanted to get laid. I would too. I knew it. I carried something now, it was like a big opening flower, it was irresistible. I was bulletproof, altitude proof, poison proof. I ran down that narrow street, I passed through a current of colour and warm air and snippets of conversation. A black woman walked toward me; she was wearing a white dress and carrying a white umbrella; the breeze ruffled the linen on her dress and the parasol gleamed like a dazzling flower in the sun.

"Hello, honey," she said.

Chapter Eleven

So I started telling anyone who would listen that I had a play on.

Teachers stopped me in the hall or the common room and asked me what's new.

"I'm writing a play," I'd say.

"What's it about?"

"It's a secret."

One day a red-haired woman approached me in the library at St. Dennis High School.

"I hear you're a playwright," she whispered. "May I ask your opinion about something?"

One night I was having a drink at the Circus when my cousin Warren wandered in. Something warned me to take it easy. But I didn't. I told him. It felt off though, like I was bragging about having sex with a girl. And I realized in mid sentence that I wanted him to tell Harrow, I wanted his cunt mother to know it too. I was going to fry them both.

But my balls went down a size overnight and I woke up flipped out. I thought, fuck, they'll go to the theatre and they'll threaten Claire and he'll fold like a fucking deck chair and I will have fucked myself because I couldn't keep my mouth shut. Because I had to brag.

I kept a low profile for a couple of days, I hardly raised my voice; somebody asked how the play was coming, I said it was on hiatus and changed the subject. Honestly, the effort not to brag seemed to hurt me physically. A few days went by and nothing happened; I poked my nose out again.

Claire Powers had done something for me with the scribble of a pen that I hadn't been able to do, ever. He had made me a writer. A real one. Because a play, or so it seemed, was not a brochure on healthy gums. It was the real thing. It was the big leagues. The truth is, I suppose, that, somewhere in my heart, I never expected it to go on. I didn't know what would go wrong, but I suspected something would.

At night, while I slept in my green room in Chinatown, I had dreams about being called up on stage to play the drums in a band with Harrow and that poor boy with the acne who played the guitar so well. They were still in their children's bodies, but I was a grown up, at least in my head. We started into a song, a straight-ahead twelve-bar blues, nice and fast. Everyone was there, Daphne and Jane and Dorothy Wilson and all the boys and girls from my old neighbourhood, when suddenly a cymbal slipped down in its stand; I righted it, then a drum went wonky, falling to the side. I held it in place with my hand; then the high hat tipped over. You see where this is going. I was all ready to play, to show everybody how good I was–and my drums keep falling apart. I had this dream over and over, a shrill voice calling out for recognition: a quality I despise.

Some days, I admit, I daydreamed that Florence Winncup would come to the play, that when it got to the part, the moment when she suggests they chop up Pascal, I saw in my black heart an image of her clutching her chest in the theatre, dying of a stroke right there on the floor, of my play literally killing her. I daydreamed of her funeral, of going out to the cemetery after the last stone had been turned, the last mourner left, of creeping up to her gravestone, of letting a big gob of spit form in my mouth, of letting it drop on to her grave. I confess, it made me happy to imagine that scenario. I never would have believed I was full of such poison, such a black desire to wound. But I was.

I imagined other things too; I imagined Harrow grabbing me by the throat on the street, I wouldn't go limp this time, I'd fight back. Besides, I wondered darkly, how likely is it for a man on a murder charge to pick a fight on the street? No, that had to be a breach of bail, fighting in a public place. I had him. I had them both.

Once I allowed myself to admit how much I loathed Harrow, suddenly I couldn't do enough to wound him.

And yet, sometimes, I felt such terror. I woke up in the middle of the night; my heart thumped with fright. I must stop this, I'd say, tomorrow I must go down to the Front Porch Theatre and pull the play.

But in the morning, when the sun was out and the trees waved in the breeze and people milled about on the sidewalk below my window, it didn't seem like such a capital crime. It was playing in a small, alternative theatre. Who would see it? What were the chances of a juror stumbling in? And if he did, he could always get himself excused. And the cops? What if they came? Cops don't go to the theatre. Anyway I could always call it spec, I made it up, why not? I'm a writer. They make things up all the time.

I figured it was safe. I just couldn't bring it down myself, just couldn't go back to not being a writer again.

I asked a lawyer at my gym what would happen if I got caught putting on the play before the trial.

"You must already know the answer to that one," he said.

"No, I don't."

"Well," he said, matter-of-factly, "you'd be in contempt of court."

"What would happen then?"

"They'd close the show, fine the theatre and throw you in jail."

I found that vaguely exhilarating, I don't know why but I did.

Three weeks later, we were in late July now, I got a call from Claire; he wanted to see something. I sent him down half the play. I waited sick with nerves. He'd called my bluff, I was sure of it, he was going to call back and say, "Look, I just read your stuff and I don't know how to say this but . . . "

Claire called back just before dinner and said, "I love it, it's genius."

Well, of course it wasn't genius; but it was better than a kick in the ass.

I went over to Kalie's. We had a glass of wine at the kitchen table. I was very happy. After a while we went into Jesse's room to tuck him in. We looked down at the sleeping little boy. Suddenly I felt fear clutch at my heart. What would happen if something happened to him?

"What is it?" Kalie said.

"Nothing."

"No, what?"

"What if something happened to him? I just don't think . . . "

"Oh, don't," she said.

I could feel her looking at me in the dark room.

"You don't have a sense or anything, do you?"

"No, I don't."

"I just don't think . . . "

"I think I'd die."

"Don't let's talk about it." We looked down at the sleeping boy and felt dizzy with love.

The next morning Claire sent me over a cheque for $750. For writing. It was fantastic.

And then one Sunday afternoon I was standing in front of a bank machine not far from my house. I was lost in thought, thinking about my play really, about a plot problem, when two arms slipped around my chest and tightened. At first it was a joke and I let out a laugh; but the grip tightened; a very strong man was squeezing me, I craned my head around and there was Harrow. He had a grim smile on his face, he appeared not to be exerting himself, or rather that's how he wanted me to perceive him. It made him scarier.

Then he relaxed his grip.

I started talking, I started going on about this and that, asking him questions, my heart beating like mad. Did he know? Did he not know? I could hardly look at him, it was so peculiar to have spent the day writing about him, as if he were dead, and suddenly there he was, in front of me, very much alive.

He narrowed his eyes and set his mouth in an expression of impatient disgust.

"Look, I talked to Warren."

I said nothing.

"What the fuck are you doing?"

"It's no big deal."

"It's a very big deal. It's a life-in-prison deal." He paused.

"Is it about Pascal?" he asked.

I said nothing.

His face blackened. "Are you out of your fucking mind? Do you want to kill me? Do you hate me? Is that what this is about?"

"I don't know anything, Harrow. I wasn't there. . . . "

He brushed it away.

"What if the cops hear about it, what if the jury hears about it, what if the newspapers hear about it? I'm fighting for my fucking life here."

He took a long careful look at me and then frowned.

"You've got to cancel it. At least until after the trial."

"I can't do that," I said.

"Look," he said, coming closer to me. "I'm not going to let you fuck me like this."

"Back off, back the fuck off." I gave him a shove. It surprised us both. "You threaten me again and I'll go straight to the cops and I'll tell them I was there. I'll tell them the whole fucking business. Now, you going to kill me too? No? All right. Now fuck off."

"Why are you doing this?"

"Because you're an asshole and I've already wasted enough of my life on you."

He looked stunned.

"You're a lousy friend, Harrow. And that was some fucking horror show you put on out there in the grass. Some fucking horror show. You brought this bullshit on yourself. You and your fucking mother."

"What are you talking about?"

"You shot the wrong person, Harrow. You should have shot your mother."

"You've got to cancel this play. I mean it. It'll kill me."

"Who shot Pascal, Harrow?"

"I did."

"Was your mother there? Don't bullshit me."

He grimaced, looked away, then opened his mouth to answer. But stopped.

"Let's keep walking, all right?"

"I'm not wearing a microphone, Harrow."

"I know," he said wearily.

I opened my shirt. "Look."

"I know," he said. He did take a look though.

Then he began.

"We were cranked. We'd been doing China White all day long, Pascal came into the living room, he swiped the bottle of Remy Martin off the fridge and guzzled it down. Then he went kind of nuts. He said he was going to chop off his cock, that he was sure it would grow back. I said that wasn't a very good idea. That he'd bleed to death. He said he didn't have any blood in his body. It was all green gas. He went back into the kitchen. He got a kitchen knife. Then the phone rang. It was Mother. Pascal picked up the phone and said I was already dead. He said that to my mother. Then he ripped the phone out of the wall and threw it in the yard. I said, put the knife down Pascal, and he said, shake me and I'll go boom. He was fucking crackers, Christian. He took a step toward me, he looked kind of cunning, he was sort of grinning, mischievously. Then my mother came in the door, blasting. I mean she must have fetched my old man's shotgun out of the cupboard, thrown it in the car and come straight over. Christ you should have seen it. Pascal turned around, knife in hand, that stupid smile on his face and boy, did he get the surprise of his life. One shot, right in the bean."

I let out a surprised laugh.

"Your mother shot him? Are you serious?"

"Kicked his ass very, very hard."

"So how did you get the brains on the wall? Because obviously Pascal wasn't standing by the wall."

"We did that later. We took a smear from his head and creamed it on the wall. Mother did. I was so stoned I couldn't make a snowball."

"Then?"

"Then we tore shit out of the place. We were going to chop him up but I must have come down; the China White must have worn off because suddenly it didn't make any sense. I knew we were going to get caught."

"So you called me?"

"I thought you'd make a better alibi. But then you wouldn't play. So we flushed the dope down the toilet, and called the cops."

"Whose idea was that?"

"Flushing the dope? It was hers," he said quietly. "She didn't want a scandal." He paused. "You've got to cancel this play. It's going to get me hanged."

"All right," I said. "All right. But only until after the trial."
He disappeared up the alley.

It's funny what happened next. I went back to my apartment; the world changed, I could see it on the way home. The sunlight was thin and cheap; unattractive people bumped me; a dog barked at me from behind a fence. My apartment looked small and messy, it looked like a loser's apartment. I turned on the television set; the babble of whores. Suddenly I realized what it was. I had nothing to look forward to any more and it sucked the life out of me like air from a balloon. The play was off, everything was over. If I cancelled it now, Claire would cancel it for good. He'd punish me. He was a small, retaliatory man.

But what if Harrow was lying to me? And then I thought of him revolving nude, fat and slug-white in that dandelion field. What if it was a lie? That was pretty good shooting for a small-town secretary. Where did she get the shells from?

Gradually I found myself wondering–or allowed myself to wonder–if in fact I'd written the play about Harrow as an act of revenge, which is what I'd imagined, or rather if revenge was merely the paint I had coated it in. Maybe I'd written the play because I had the opportunity to and had justified it by heating up old quarrels with Harrow. Could a birthday party have been so important? What then was the point? The point was, I guessed, that I was desperate to get something going in my life, desperate not to be a supply teacher forever. And now the prospect of going back on it, it was simply too depressing to contemplate.

Confused, I looked out the window at the booby hatch. The phone rang, it was Claire; he was calling about some tidbit about the play, a casting option. I listened carefully, I knew I had to say it now or it was lost, I was never going to say it. And I didn't. I just let it slip by like a dream. When I put the phone down, the play was on again.

I planned on going to the gym. I'd lift weights, run around

the track; I'd get fit and by the time the play went on, well, I'd be ready, no matter what. I slunk around for a few days. I didn't want anything to go wrong. I just wanted the fucking play to go up, even if it had only one performance, I just wanted to say one time in my life that I had a play on, I wrote it, it got produced, and fuck you. I think I might have even prayed too. You know, God let this happen, just once. Sometimes I felt a little sick with nerves, as if I had a hangover, as if the sheer ugliness in my personality was poisoning me.

I didn't hear from Harrow again. I rehearsed a lot of speeches and when I thought about him and my childhood and his fucking mother I got pissed off again; convenient perhaps, I still don't know. But I didn't hear anything. Sometimes Claire rang and I waited, blood pumping furiously in my head, for him to say something bad, something like we're cancelling the play, but he didn't. It was all just business stuff. Claire was an asshole, I knew that, but by now the play was strapped to his self-interest; that makes anyone trustworthy. He called to talk about actors and this and that, he called sometimes just to make himself feel important.

Because I was grateful to him, because I needed him, it sort of transformed him. Sometimes he seemed wonderful, likable, gifted, courageous.... I was like one of those fucking actors I'd seen in the after-hours bar. All deference and chuckles because this goof could do something for me. I tread softly around him, kind of sucked up to him and he liked that and every so often he'd call up just to get a little hit of it.

But he *was* an asshole. I mean, imagine this: We were workshopping the play, it was early morning, there were new actors on the set. Claire put on a Bob Marley tape, lit up a joint and did a kind of silly reggae walk across the stage, talking in Jamaican patois. It made me want to hide my head. I imagined Harrow seeing it, like a gargoyle up in the corner of the theatre, and I felt ashamed.

One day, during an audition, an actress playing Florence said, "Wow, these are awful people." It was a curious, flat statement. It made me think. There was very little exaggeration in the play. I kind of spilled the Winncups into the sandbox and let them amuse themselves. And they came out thus.

"Yes, they are," Claire said, giving me a wide-eyed smile.

"Are they like . . . real people?"

Claire loved this, the intrigue.

"Let's not get into that," he snapped. The actress looked down, reconsidered her tack.

"No," she said slowly, "but I need to know. Are they just like this now? Or have they always been like that?"

So I invented a bit of business about Florence hiring Warren to burn down the family antique store–just to let the audience know that on that fall day when the windows turned blue and Pascal's face flew away, the Winncups had not, how shall I put it, acted out of character.

"I don't know," said the actress thoughtfully, "they seem like people the Borgias wouldn't want to have lunch with."

And then the photograph arrived. I got a letter in the mail. I opened it up and there it was: a picture of me, ass naked, tied to a bed, with a girl standing beside me with a whip. It was a bit of silliness I got involved in when I was in university, many drinks, many drugs, and it kind of happened. Harrow was there; in fact what the picture didn't show was him tied up, bare assed, beside me. But that part of the picture was missing; it had been snipped away.

I looked at the photo, I flipped it over, there was no note, nothing on the back. But I was sure it wasn't from Harrow. That just wasn't his style. No, it was his mother. I was sure.

Still it spooked me. For half a day I imagined what I was supposed to imagine, that she'd send the photograph to the theatre, that Claire would take one look at it and can the play. He was after all part politician. "I can't do a play with a guy like this," he'd say. "The chicks'd be all over me." And that'd be that. I'd try other theatres, they'd get the same picture in the mail, I'd be fucked. I'd go for a teaching job, the guy would open my file and there it'd be, that fucking picture. *I'm afraid we can't hire you to rake the leaves here, not if this is the sort of activity you get up to in your leisure time.*

But I held on. I was getting the hang of these Winncups. And I was right. Nothing happened.

That wasn't the end of it. Near the middle of August, I got a call from Dorian; she said she was at the airport, that she had to talk to me about something. I said sure and she turned up at my door about twenty minutes later. We went out for a drink; I smoked a cigarette, which I hadn't done in years. Then I was necking with her, there in the bar, she had her tongue in my mouth, I hurried her out, we came back to my place, we stopped in the dark foyer, I have to go, she said, standing very close to me, not moving. She melted into my arms like toffee, she had a body like that, it just folded into yours, she smelt lovely. I pulled my head back, I felt in the dark for her lips and I found them, sweet and tentative, I was just frantic with excitement for her, I found myself wanting to say the most extraordinary things to her, things I'd never said to a woman before. She slipped down on to her knees and put my cock in her mouth. I was hers. Period.

"Tell me what you want," I said.

I took her upstairs, I undressed her with shaking hands, she lay down on the bed, she had a long creamy body, very white. Then I bent down and gave her a blow job and honestly she tasted so good and so tender, I wanted it to go on forever....

"Here," she said, "here, let me show you something."

And before long she was lying there, tied to the bed posts with my father's old school ties and slippery with coconut oil.

Then she was in the shower. I lay there feeling as if I should go to confession and she came out of the bathroom and handed me a cigarette and I said no, no, and then she said, still naked, look, don't go all dark on me, it's just me, all right, nothing special. Then she called a cab. She gave me a peck on the cheek. I came back upstairs and I undid the oily ties and I threw them in the sink and I ran some hot water and I threw in some soap and I watched, glassy-eyed, as the water rose up and swallowed the ties.

I'd been had, I knew that but I wasn't sure how. I didn't know what the tab was, not yet. I expected her to call the next day but she didn't; then I expected her to call the day after but she didn't. And my not wanting to see her got a little fainter, my self-disgust faded away, and by the end of a week, when I thought of that long creamy body on my bed, I found myself sitting beside the phone hoping it would ring. But it didn't. It was the strangest thing. I was mighty intrigued, mighty horny too and I called her at her apartment, I was going to leave a message on the answering machine but I went cold at the beep, I had a sense of real danger. I just held on to the line so that when she got home she would know that there was someone who called her, who waited on the line, who deliberately didn't leave a message. She'd know it was me.

But still she didn't call.

And a week later I knew it was over. It was suddenly very clear. She didn't fuck me to get the play cancelled. She fucked me to do in her mother. What better way to do it?

Quite a bunch, those Winncups, just full of surprises.

It was September again. They were green, green mornings, the students milled along the street under my window, knapsacks on their backs, in groups of five and six, clusters of them, skirts and shirttails and brown legs and white shirts and ties.

Then the play opened. On opening night, just before the curtain came up, I went for a long walk. I walked along the north side of the street, I saw someone I knew, I waved at them like a sleepwalker. I walked and walked and walked. I felt terribly sad, sad for the world, sad for a girl sitting in a car, sad for a bartender, wiping his rag on the table, sad for John Lennon, sad for children whose mothers were mean to them, sad for a cab driver clicking down his meter, sorry for the washerwoman, sorry for the operator, sorry for the subway driver blowing his whistle, sorry for the street sweeper ... sorry for myself. I realized I was nervous, drop-dead nervous and it was passing itself off as a kind of weltschmerz.

I went back to the theatre. I slipped through the crowd. It smelt heavenly, like money and perfume, like one of my mother's parties when I did the honours with Harrow. You could hear the jewellery rattle, but the perfume, it suggested such romance. Kalie came and stood beside me. She wore just a little too much rouge on her cheeks. I held her hand. Her long fingers were cool, they felt powdered.

"I'm going to go get my seat," she said.

Then I went backstage. I peeked through the curtains. There were only seventy-five seats but they were sold out, if that's the word for a papered house. I saw a critic from *The Globe and Mail.* I didn't see Harrow or his mother or the red-haired cop. I don't think I could have stood it. I saw people sitting down, the show was almost ready to go. I looked at the faces, I realized there were no old friends in the crowd, no one I'd known longer than five years. Where did they all go? Donald and Randall and Laurie and Frank and Anne and Bill–and Harrow. There was a time when we were inseparable. They were the people I wanted to see this. But they were all gone, they were no longer a part of my life.

The door to the theatre closed, the house got very quiet, I felt dizzy as if I were going to faint. I went around to the front of the house, I tiptoed past the box office; a man with a small, round face which shone like a nickel ran across the street and into the theatre. They ushered him in.

The show began.

There was a terrible strained silence; I heard an actor's voice through the door. It was the woman playing Mrs. Winncup. They were talking about the store. About burning it down.

"I think we should dispose of it, dear," she said.

Someone laughed; it was Kalie.

There was a party afterwards. I tried not to drink too much; it was my very first play, I knew it was unrepeatable, I wanted to savour it. So I stayed sober at the party. People bought me beers; I accepted them graciously, put them down in the shadows and left them there. A trio of high-school teachers from Bickford Park came; they wanted to meet the actors. It was very exciting for them.

I don't dance very well so I didn't dance at the party, but everyone else did; Claire, the teachers, Kalie, Spolin and his new wife, the critic from *The Globe and Mail*–a good sign, Kalie said, because he never dances at parties for plays he doesn't like. But she was blasted by then and I took it with a grain of salt; in fact, I pretended not to hear it. I didn't want to jinx anything.

The man with the shiny face came over. "I liked your play, Mr. Blackwood," he said. "I know people just like that."

Then, when no one was looking, I slipped out. It was a Friday night. Chinatown burned with life, flashing dragons, orange exploding cats. Glazed pigs hung from hooks in windows. The smell of grease and meat cooked over an open flame gusted out on to the street; it drifted across the park and up the wall of my house. Couples in light spring coats walked along the sidewalk, hand in hand.

I wandered on under the moon. On and on and on. I stopped in front of a big, airy Caribbean bar. I went in. It was dark in there, the ceiling a soft green; through the skylight I saw the moon had followed me into the room.

A reggae band, six black guys, dreadlocks swelling their toques so their heads looked like spring flowers ready to burst into bloom, honked and strutted and walked and grooved through "Night Nurse." Horns glowed like treasures, congas like fat, gaudy children. I saw a picture of Harrow and me dancing in a bar by the ocean at four o'clock in the morning: just the two of us, weaving around an empty floor while an overproof drunk snoozed on a table and the fishermen got ready to go out to sea.

I ordered a Mexican beer. It came from a bucket. It was ice-cold and I drank it quickly. It tasted great. I ordered another. The bartender bought it for me.

"I'll put a couple more on ice for you," he said. I must have had that look. At the far end of the bar a coloured television flashed mutely, a pleasant harmless bauble. An aging rounder came in. He was wearing a pressed white shirt, tight jeans, cowboy boots, his blond hair slicked back. I recognized him. I didn't know him but I didn't like him. It depressed me vaguely to see him. He stood in the doorway, checked quickly and impersonally over the crowd, kissed a waitress, his eyes never stopped working the crowd. But after a while, the shadows pulled back and I forgot about him and the room filled with excitement. Perspiring girls pushed through the smoke and the music and one of them smiled at me and kept moving and the horns blasted a single, strident note and the band swung into "Fire." The whole bar seemed to catch the rhythm, the bartender picked it up, the bus boy picked it up, a beautiful waitress with thick dark hair and a sleeveless shirt picked it up. The band kicked the song up a key, the excitement went up, it was like a spirit, it just soared, you could almost see it, and the waitress put down her tray and put her hands in the air and swung her hips, side to side, rocked them back and forth–it was just the tip, just enough to let you know she was a breathlessly good dancer. Something magic, something ineffable poured up through the ceiling straight up at the moon and I realized, or I caught myself realizing–I was happy.

Chapter Twelve

The critic who adored my play subsequently killed himself with a handful of phenobarbital and a gin chaser, but at the time, the morning the review appeared, he seemed at the top of his swing.

It gave me a kick an adult shouldn't require. I walked for hours nursing the sensation like a chocolate in my palm. When I saw a man in a bowler hat step into a restaurant with the newspaper under his arm, I thought in a few moments he'll open the paper, flip through it and then he'll be reading about me. All over the city, all over the country, people will be reading about me.

Goodness gracious.

I ran into Paul Bouissac that day, a professor from the university. Harrow and I had taken his surrealism course. "You look younger," he said, with French irony, as if somehow looking young was a bourgeois ailment. "You look . . . " he searched for the word, "*arrivé.*"

I wrote a note to the critic. I didn't give a shit if it was bad form. I said thanks for your review, it gave me an embarrassing amount of pleasure. Then I got another good review. Someone said reviewers were always generous to first-time playwrights but I figured they were just jealous. It only lasted a couple of hours, the kick that is.

After two weeks I was used to being a playwright. Like a coke addict I needed another hit. One night I was sitting in the Epicure with Claire.

"You know," I said, "it's a pity we can't get that cunt, Florence, to the show."

A moment later, I got down off the stool, I went to the house phone and called her number.

She answered on the second ring.

"I got your letter," I said. "The one with the photo."

I could feel her thinking.

"But that's not why I called," I went on. "I'd like you to come and see something. I'd like you to come and see my play. There's something in it just for you."

"Is there, Christian?"

"It's a sort of belated present from my mother."

That stopped both of us. Until the words came from my mouth, I had no idea what they'd be.

"What do you think your mother would make of this . . . " she looked for the word, "situation?"

"I don't honestly know, Florence, but I do know there's a hell of a show you should see."

I put down the phone. I was still laughing but it felt like a stupid laugh, it felt as if I had been outclassed. I wondered for a second, too, if she *had* sent me the photograph. Maybe the whole thing was an appalling, dangerous, irresponsible mistake.

A few nights later, she came. I knew she would. I understood how the organism worked now. She arrived at the last moment. There was a ticket waiting for her in her name. But she didn't take it. She bought her own.

She sat near the back of the theatre. I watched her through a crack in the set. The lights went down, the play began. At first, she watched impassively, there was no reaction at all. But near the end of the scene she opened her purse and took out a small notebook and a pad and she began to make notes. She knew I was watching her. What was she writing? Was she bluffing? What was she going to do with the notes?

A stagehand came over and tapped me on the shoulder. I was in the way, she wanted to get the exploding head ready. I helped her move a table; when I peeked back at the audience, Florence's seat was empty; she was gone. There was a hole where she had been. I hurried around to the front of the theatre. The street was empty; she must have caught a taxi or stepped into a restaurant.

Then, at the top of the street, a pair of red tail lights flashed soundlessly on. Smoke rose behind the car. I walked very slowly toward it. I knew who was in the car; she must have caught sight of me because the car didn't move. Florence sat in the interior of the Thunderbird staring straight ahead.

I went over and stood beside the car, a little ways back. I wondered if she had a gun. It spooked me the way she just sat there, completely still. I knocked on the window. She turned her head very slowly and looked at me. Then there was the purr of the window going down. I could see both her hands, I could see the emerald ring. I lowered my head to the window.

"So," I said, "how did you like the show?"

She looked at me coolly.

"How long is this going to go on, Christian?" she said.

"Until you're dead, Florence. Dead and in the ground." The window purred up. I stepped out of the way and watched the car pull on to the quiet street. I confess this business with Harrow's mother has always troubled me. Was it jealousy perhaps, jealousy that in a competition with her I never won? She was a bad, awful, dangerous woman. I said it when I was a kid and I'm still saying it, even though to see her now, she is a small, stooped woman. But she ruined those children, Harrow and his sister Dorian.

They never had a chance. I say this now, knowing how it must sound. I think Harrow was a great man whose legs were crippled at birth. He was a bright, strong, beautiful kid and I think his mother knew, seconds after she saw those sinewy bloody arms, those strong legs, that he was going to wander far afield unless she stopped him. And so she fixed him. That was the kind of woman she was. If it sounds as if I still hate her after all these years, I don't. But to this day I think she should be put to death for the evil she did her children.

You might think God would punish me for my sins, but he didn't. A week after the play closed, a guy I didn't like phoned and asked if I wanted to audition for a new television show. They needed a music critic, a fresh face, he said. So that night, I went to see a Dutch reggae band, cribbed part of my review from an old *Boston Globe* and went in the next day for the audition. A few hours later a woman with a pretty mouth called up and asked if I wanted the job. I said sure. It was like being asked if you want to be the mayor of Philadelphia. I said sure, yeah, and the next thing I knew I was the mayor of Philadelphia. This business with Harrow, the ripples just went on and on and on. It was like he should have killed someone a lot earlier. For my sake anyway.

Then the little boy came to stay with me.

His mother had met a celebrated Renaissance professor and, in the dwindling days of fall, he'd invited her to come for a ten-day canoe trip through Algonquin Park. I don't think Kalie had ever read Milton or been on a canoe trip before but she went. One bright morning, a car with a big green canoe stopped in front of my house and a little boy spilled out.

That night, at five in the morning, it started: a small, insistent cough. I went into his room and rubbed his neck. The coughing stopped. I went back to bed; it started again. I must have been more unstable than I thought because, lying there in the darkness, I began to imagine dreadful things, dreadful daydreams, half awake, half asleep, about something happening to him. And all the time, that cough.

Then it stopped.

That morning, he was exhausted; so was I, but I had a jazz film to screen at ten o'clock. I couldn't get hold of his babysitter so I had to take him to school. He cried on the way there; it made me guilty, then impatient, then I snapped at him. We had a reconciliation in the hall and then I dropped him off in his classroom.

In the afternoon, after school, I bundled him up and took him to the park but I couldn't shake off the malaise, a sense that something was wrong, a sense that I'd done something wrong. Left a stove on, been mean to someone, lost my keys, bounced an important cheque, what was it? I thought I saw omens everywhere. A man carrying a wolf-puppy in his arms; a blood-filled syringe in the grass, pigeons swarming like maggots at the foot of a tree.

Jesse sat on my lap. We were watching a little boy his age swinging on a swing, his shadow skimming over the cold sand. Suddenly the sun disappeared, the wind picked up, it rattled the leaves. It sent a shiver over me. You could smell winter. When I looked again the swing was empty. The little boy had vanished. I looked around. He wasn't on the monkey bars, he wasn't in the sandbox; he didn't seem to be in the park anymore. I wondered how much time had elapsed. I don't know why but I reached over and slipped my hand under Jesse's shirt. I listened for a heartbeat. I needed the reassurance of it. His small chest was very warm, but so frail, so unprotected. Why didn't little boys have stronger bones? They were the ones who needed them. I looked at his wrists, his skull, his eyes, it was as if he were made of the most beautiful glass in the world.

That night he ran a light fever. I wondered whether I should call his grandmother out in the Prairies. No, that would start a chain reaction. I contemplated calling Kalie's answering machine but I changed my mind.

We had a quiet dinner, a tub, a story, then he went to bed again. He laid his head on the pillow. I left on the light. I read

Graham Greene in his room. I can't remember the book, just the image of a vulture perching on a tin roof. I noticed Jesse had fallen asleep so I covered him in his Batman blanket and went to bed. I looked at myself in the bedroom mirror. Had I been drinking too much? What was the matter with me? What was bugging me?

That night the cough returned. It woke me up like a rock thrown through the window. I checked the clock. Five o'clock again. I went into his room and he reached up a little arm; it looked so thin, so pale, that I caught myself thinking, My God, he's dying, he's dying.

Near dawn, he rolled over and a little drop of blood trickled down his lips. I gathered him up and called a taxi and took him down to the hospital. We sat in the emergency room. The coughing stopped. But I didn't go home. Around sunrise, a bearded doctor came out and took us into a bright yellow examining room. He looked down the little boy's throat with a long stick, he felt his glands, he tapped his tummy.

He took some blood; there was a fuss, but he gave him the needle anyway.

"He popped a little vessel in his throat," the doctor said. "It's not uncommon."

And then we went home. I put him in my bed and he fell asleep at once.

The next night, I heard a dreadful sound, a quiet muffled sound. When I went into his room, the little boy had his head under the covers; he was trying to cough so I wouldn't hear him because he didn't want to go back to the hospital.

"Am I going to get another needle?" he cried.

He lay still for a while, then a cough, then another, then silence. And each time I thought that's it, that's the last time. And then he coughed again. I was transported by morbid daydreams, they played themselves out like movies. I imagined the phone call with his mother, would I tell her on the phone, would I go to her house? Where would I leave his body?

He must have felt something because at one point he raised

an arm up and touched me. Sitting beside his bed, I started to imagine that God was punishing me, that he was going to take my son away from me because I'd done something terrible, because I'd betrayed my childhood friend, because I'd been arrogant enough to think I'd gotten away with it. And now he was going to show me. I started to believe that a pestilence had been sent down, had been visited upon me. And I caught myself praying, caught myself whispering in the dark room, *"If you stop him coughing, if you make him better, I'll make it up, I will, I promise."*

I made that promise to the dark room.

But it didn't stop the coughing. I couldn't stand it. It made me want to cut myself, I had to do something, move. I picked him up and took him into my bed and in a little while, he calmed down.

I kept him home from school the next day. I skipped an interview. I could make it up later. But the unsmiling producer called me at home. I told her about the little boy.

"Oh," she said. "All right."

I'm not sure she believed me, but she had a child herself, couldn't bring herself, I think, not to give me the benefit of the doubt. I was very tired, I needed sleep but I couldn't get any. I cleaned the kitchen, I did the laundry, I stripped his bed, the sheets, the pillow slip, and took it downstairs. The little boy woke up near noon and we spent the day playing cards, watching a video, waiting for nightfall.

Around 8:30 I put him to bed. I was exhausted, barely able to read him a story. He coloured in his colouring book for a while, lying on his stomach and then he fell asleep. I crawled into bed. I watched the news, then turned out the light. My heart was racing, but when I tried to get up, when I even thought of getting up, a kind of nauseating weariness poured down on me. I lay on my side, staring through a crack in the blinds at a street light. Tiny strings of orange floated across my eyeball.

I looked at the clock. It wasn't even midnight. I'd be awake all night. I'd wait till five o'clock and then I'd take him back to the hospital. I'd call his mother. I'd go to church. I'd call Harrow.

I'd go and see Frank Sinatra. Jesse and I would sit on a sunny green lawn at Lake Tahoe, the mountains rising up in the distance, a boat puttering on the lake, him playing at my feet. Everybody's there, Sonny, Freddy. Jesse's a baby again, Kalie, look: We get to have him twice, he's dressed in a white bonnet, his little fat legs popping from diapers. My, what muscular legs he has, what delicious little lamb chops, a butterball baby. God, how lucky we are to have such a divine creature.

Fly me to the moon
Let me play among the stars.

And then the horns come in.

I woke up wide-awake. It was freezing in my room, like a morgue. I grabbed my clock; my glasses fell to the floor. I stuck the clock close to my face. It was after six. The house was freezing. I looked out the windows. Frost cupped the windows. The lawns gleamed. A window rattled in the wind. There was no noise from Jesse's room, not a peep. I hurried down the hall. He lay spread-eagled on his back, the sheets and blankets on the floor, his pyjama top open, a wind blowing in through the open window. The floor felt like cold marble.

"Jesse," I said.

I hurried over to him. I put my hand on his chest. His skin was cold. I shook him and he stirred sleepily; he moved his lips and muttered about a lost toy train and sank back down into his dream. I felt for his heart. I could feel it beating, it was strong and even. I covered him up. I stood staring down at him. I looked at the clock again. After six. Something had happened. I walked back down the still hallway. Something nagged at me. It was close to the surface, I almost had it, there it was. *"I think my allergies drove him away. He was a lovely-smelling man who lived in a ragweed field. I cried all the time. Nothing would stop it. Except a frost."*

Dorian Winncup. She had told me that story the night I ran into her at Harrow's loft.

Jesse slept through the next night and the next, through all the remaining nights until his mother came home. And by the time she did, the whole thing seemed not like a memory but like a drugged episode that stood lopsided in relation to the rest of the time. And that deal I made with God, I tried to forget about it, but I couldn't quite, and one afternoon months later I came home from work early and found a strange cat lying on the little boy's pillow. He scrambled off the bed and shot out the window. I lowered the screen behind him. It seemed like a sign.

Chapter Thirteen

Harrow's trial began that spring; it was early May, almost a year to the day after the death of Pascal Charleville. That's very fast for a trial, particularly if a man is not in custody, but Harrow's lawyer belonged to a kind of legal old boy's club and he got it going early. I followed it in the newspapers. From the start it was like watching a ship go down with a man shackled to the deck. There was police testimony, a numbing recitation of evidence, the torn-up floorboards, the stripped body, the kerosene-soaked clothes, the four-hour delay before phoning the police. What happened during those four hours, the prosecution wondered? More testimony from the forensics expert who had experimented on a pig's head: the trajectory of the brain tissue, on impact, was all wrong. There were reports of Harrow's behaviour on arrest, stories of him washing his foot in the toilet while giving a statement. A report quoting him saying, "Pascal

Charleville paid the ultimate price for messing up my room."

Even now, that sentence makes me smile. But why would he have said that to the police? It was like a man begging to be sent away, begging to be put out of his misery.

It looked very bad indeed for Harrow.

One spring morning I sat in my leafy foyer overlooking the street. I had the day off, I was preparing to interview Leonard Cohen the next morning. But then very suddenly I got up and went downstairs and drove to the courthouse. It took me about twenty minutes. I parked the car and went into the white stone building; walked down a row of courts, stopped at the information desk and asked for the Winncup courtroom. It was courtroom eight. I slipped in.

Florence Winncup was on the stand. I sat quietly at the back. I looked over. I saw Tom Murphy near the front. Zinta was there but no Warren, which was strange. Harrow sat with his attorney. His mother wore a dark dress and a simple plain white scarf. She talked in the voice of a fragile old woman. I looked at the jury. They had been there for almost three weeks; they seemed half asleep, barely listening. At one point Harrow looked around and caught sight of me. He gave me a short, sharp smile and it sent a wave of guilt through me. He had cut his hair short, it accentuated the size of his face; he wore a brown suit, very large. He looked puffy.

"Where do you live?" the crown prosecutor asked Florence. He was a thin, persistent man, Mr. Robert Crosby.

"I live in Callington," Florence said.

"Do you live alone?" he asked mechanically.

She hesitated just a heartbeat.

"Yes," she said.

They got to the killing.

It was quite a performance. When she talked about Pascal holding a knife to her throat, her voice cracked, broke, her little hand shook. The judge, who should have known better, looked down sympathetically and asked her if she needed a recess.

"It's all right," she said bravely. "I'll do it. I'll finish."

Honestly, I wanted to snort out loud. I had to keep it to myself. Harrow looked over at me impassively. I looked around the courtroom. Where was Warren? Florence soldiered on.

"Why didn't you have any blood on your dress?" the crown asked.

"I don't know," she said.

"Where were you?"

"He was behind me." Here, a little shudder.

"How far behind?"

"Right behind me."

"Well, if there were brains on the wall behind you, why wasn't there some tissue or blood on your dress?"

"I don't know. I was in a moment of pure horror. I quite fainted away."

Nothing in the world could make that bitch faint away. I checked to see how it was playing with the jury. They were buying it.

It was confusing. Some moments I wanted Harrow to get away with it; others, sometimes only moments later, I wanted to throw up my hand, to leap to my feet and say, they're getting away! Can't you see that? They're getting away!

They broke for recess. I was dying for a pee. I ran into Harrow in the washroom. He stood beside me at the urinal.

"Boy," he said.

"They didn't lay a glove on you," I said. It was a stupid thing to say but when I saw him there in the flesh, I wanted, suddenly, to do something, say something to make him feel better. His brow arched up, a little boy's face appeared and he said, all full of hope and fright, "You figure?"

I could have wept for him. Wept for us both really, for what wonderful little creatures we once were. But I didn't say anything. I watched him zip up and go over to the mirror and look at himself. A wave of self-consciousness seemed to come over him; he straightened his shoulders, he looked at his teeth, he pushed down on his hair. It was like watching a child go to war.

An hour later, the court rose to its feet and we resumed. Florence was back on the stand. Mr. Crosby began a line of questioning about money, about real estate, about her late husband's lumber business; it seemed fuzzy and unfocused, I couldn't see where it was going. How many cars did she have, where was her house in relation to Harrow's? Somewhere in the middle of things I found myself drifting off. It's funny how you can get used to almost anything, even your best friend being on trial for murder.

I found myself daydreaming about Dorian Winncup. She sat near the front of the court, slightly to the side, wearing a grey dress and slowly, methodically turning a strand of hair around her finger while she listened to the testimony. I saw her spreadeagled on my bed, her hands tied to bedposts while I kissed the inside of her thigh. Suddenly, I remembered the photograph of me, the torn one that had arrived in the mail. How could I have not realized it before? It wasn't Florence who sent that photograph, it was her daughter, Dorian. And possibly, quite possibly, it had nothing whatsoever to do with blackmail.

"Mrs. Winncup," the prosecutor said suddenly, "do you own a store?"

"Yes, I do. I did."

"You did own an antique store?"

Something warned me to pay attention.

"Yes."

"You don't anymore?"

"No, Mr. Crosby, I don't."

"Why not?" he asked without interest.

Mrs. Winncup frowned, as though she had been wounded by a painful memory. It was for the jury's benefit.

"We lost it," she said quietly.

"What happened to it?"

"It burnt down."

"I see." A pause. "How did that happen?"

"I don't know what you mean, Mr. Crosby."

"That must have been a real loss."

"Yes, it was."

"A loss of income?"

"Yes, it was."

"How was the store doing?" The judge shifted uncomfortably.

"Very well, Mr. Crosby."

He let silence speak for his response.

"Did you have insurance?"

"Yes, I did."

"That's very fortunate, isn't it?"

"Yes, it was."

"Do you know a Warren Masterson?"

Florence knit her brow. Death approached. It came right up and stood beside her.

"He's a friend of my son's."

"He's a friend of your son's?"

"Yes, Mr. Crosby."

"A friend of your son's?"

Her mask slipped. "Why do you keep repeating what I say, Mr. Crosby?"

Mr. Crosby appeared not to have heard her.

"Is he a friend of yours?" he continued in the same monotone.

"A friend of mine. Well, I don't know, I suppose so. Yes."

Mr. Crosby paused a moment, found his place in the long list of written questions.

"Did you hire Mr. Masterson to burn down your store for the insurance money?"

Harrow's lawyer rose quickly to his feet, the expensive suit falling with hardly a wrinkle over his well-fed body.

"I object," he said in a rich baritone.

"This has to do directly with the credibility of a key witness," Mr. Crosby said with a humourless laugh.

The judge scowled. Mr. Crosby proceeded.

"Are you aware, Mrs. Winncup, that Mr. Masterson has already made a statement to the police to that effect; has already, in fact, signed an affidavit saying that you paid him a sum of one thousand dollars to burn down the store? I have the affidavit right here, Mrs. Winncup, if you'd like to see it."

Across the very quiet room a plump man with a shiny face pondered me expressionlessly. It was the man from the theatre.

Harrow sank back into his seat. His mother sat very straight in her chair, as if she had a chill. Her lips twitched; but there was no getting up after this one. Everyone in the court knew it. From here on, the jury would listen, they'd sleep, they'd fantasize, and then they'd go into a panelled room and a day or two days later, however long it legitimately took, they'd come out with a verdict of guilty. And Harrow would stand beside his lawyer, and the judge would sentence him to the mandatory twenty-five years in prison with no possibility of parole for ten years. His life, in a word, was over.

A recess was called. Outside it was obscenely sunny. Leaves jumped and preyed against the courthouse wall. I got into my car and drove straight to the bar.

It was late when I got home that night. I was quite drunk, I'd quarrelled with someone. I came up the stairs, I closed the curtains and sat at the kitchen table; then I got up and went down the hall and pulled out a handful of my diaries. I picked a bunch from 1968, when Harrow and I shared an apartment on Major Street, near the university.

There was a bottle of scotch on the fridge. I poured myself a deep shot. I hate scotch so I had to gag it down. It sent a shiver of nausea through me.

Upstairs, the new tenants played a slow church dirge, it was like a Gregorian chant, it was like the wrath of God being visited upon me. I remembered a time when Harrow and I were little boys and I helped him over the garden wall of his girlfriend's house; of nights running through the fog in Forest Hill; of watching him flay at the bongos in the third floor of that great big house on Dunvegan Road.

Sometime later I went for a long walk. I walked across the bridge into the Greek section of town. I walked by the Omonia, then by Kalie's. I kept going. Then I was on a dark, narrow street and in a little while I arrived at the house with the thick curtains. I went slowly up the stairs, I listened at the door, I heard nothing. I tapped the door with my knuckles. . . .

No one answered. A light went off behind the heavy curtains. I knocked again.

"Harrow," I said to the door. "Harrow."

There was no sound.

"Harrow," I said. "Harrow!"

The door opened a crack. His face looked out.

"What is it?" he said.

"Let me in," I said.

"It's too late," he said. The door closed.

"Harrow," I said.

The door opened. He looked out. It felt as if there was someone in the room with him.

"It's too late," he said.

"No, it isn't."

"It is."

"There's got to be something."

He opened the door and I stepped into the thick darkness. I smelt perfume. We walked across the living-room carpet and into the bedroom.

I saw a suitcase pushed partially under the bed.

"You're leaving?" I asked.

He looked evenly at me, then said: "I need some I.D."

"I thought you said they left you your passport."

"They did. But I don't want to risk going through a computer in Toronto. I might turn up on it."

"Do you want mine?" I said after a moment.

"Is it clean? Are you sure?"

"Yes."

"No traffic tickets, nothing?"

"Nothing."

Then the bathroom door opened and his mother came out.

"Hello, Christian," she said.

"Hello, Florence."

Harrow drove me back to my apartment. We came quietly up the stairs and went down the hall into my study and I yanked open the filing cabinet.

"Come with me," he said.

"Where?" I said.

He pulled out his wallet, opened it up and took out a clipping from the newspaper. He handed it to me.

"Read that," he said. It was a brief announcement, in a box, dated a couple of weeks previously. I only read the headline: *Trinidad drops passport requirements for Commonwealth citizens.*

"Are you going to Trinidad?"

"I am now."

"When?"

"Tomorrow. Morning."

"You'll be extradited in a week."

"I'm going to fly out of there. I'll use your I.D. to get into the country and then I'll fly out. I won't turn up in *their* computers."

"Why there?"

"Because it's seven miles from South America. I'm almost there."

I was going through plastic bags, old bills, phone records, pictures of my family, when I came across the brown wallet my father had given me when I was fourteen. I opened it. There was a heart, a small tiny heart drawn in ink in the lower left-hand corner, with the name Daphne under it. I'd forgotten. I was in love with Daphne in those days. And Harrow was in love with Jane. Inside I found a birth certificate with a splash of toothpaste on the upper right-hand corner, a social insurance card, an unsigned credit card for a local shopping mall, a card for the supply teacher's union, also unsigned.

"You're in luck," I said. I handed him the bunch. He took them and with those careful fingers shuffled slowly through them. His face relaxed.

"This is terrific," he said. "Really terrific."

"Listen, I've got Xeroxes of my diplomas, do you want them?"

He thought for a moment.

"No. Yes. Sure, why not?"

"Where are you going to go after Trinidad?"

"Don't know," he said.

"No really, I won't tell anyone."

"Don't know."

"Rio?"

"Maybe." He looked at the floor.

After a moment I said, "Are you going alone?"

He nodded.

"Christ."

"I'm fucked if I stay," he said. He looked around the room and exhaled heavily. "I knew that store was a bad-news bear but I sure didn't expect it to come back like this. Fuck me doodle."

"Harrow, I *never*..." My voice wavered.

He looked at me through round, red-rimmed eyes.

"I got to go."

I stood up. I waited for him to do something. But he surprised me.

"Want to come with me?" he asked again. "Just to the border." It sounded almost mischievous. At least that's how I remember it. Like someone asking you to pour them a martini at nine o'clock in the morning.

"What?"

"Come with me. Just for the beginning."

"I can't, Harrow, I've got to interview Leonard Cohen in the morning." I could have said something worse but I can't imagine what it could have been. It was like rubbing his face in it, in all of it.

"Just for company."

"Can't. I've got to work." He nodded.

"Right," he said. He said it crisply and it shamed me. He shifted his weight. He wouldn't look at me. He started to turn away.

"No, wait," I said.

"We'll go through separate wickets."

"I don't have any money."

"Believe me," he said hoarsely and with tremendous feeling, "dough is not the problem."

After a moment he said, "What are you smiling about?" I was thinking about those fantasies I had when I was a kid, the moment where I throw the grappling hook high up over the castle wall and reach down and pull up my friend Harrow; that night in my parents' house, all those years ago, up in the yellow study, reading a sonnet and pacing the room in a fever.

But if the while I think on thee, dear friend
All losses are restored and sorrows end.

"I'm smiling, Harrow Winncup, because I have known you for a very, very long time."

"I bet you never thought it would end like this."

End? Is it possible for it to end with someone you know like that? Is there a last day or a last moment? When the light goes out on the universe, it goes out for the person who created it with you, too. Surely.

He went back down the stairs.

At 4:35 in the morning, the limo pulled to a stop in front of my house. A single bird harped in a tree. I waved from the foyer and went quickly down the stairs. The driver popped the trunk, I threw in my bag and I got in the back seat. It was cool and leather-smelling in there; jazz filtered though expensive speakers.

"We're off to see the wizard," Harrow said. He was slumped against the door. But he was straight, I could tell that. He wasn't drunk and he wasn't stoned. It was a bit late coming but it seemed, for the moment anyway, that Harrow Winncup had caught hold of the rope.

The limo slid to the end of the street.

"There's somewhere I want to go first," he said, and we turned up through Chinatown. The dragons and the exploding cats slept. An Oriental man stacked cardboard boxes on the sidewalk. A street cleaner drove by, its brushes whirring against the cement.

"I always wanted to get a job doing that," Harrow said. It was, as they say, something to say. We drove up through the quiet city. Chet Baker hummed in the background.

Almost me,
Almost you,
Almost blue.

He wound down the window as if to get closer to the street signs, the street corners, the stores, the marquees, the city he'd grown up in. The air smelt fragrant, perfumed. We both smelt it at the same time. "Do you smell that?" he said. "What is that, what is that smell?" It needed a name. He wanted to hold on to it.

"Lilacs," I said.

"Lilacs," he said softly. His back was to me and I wondered if he was crying.

"I just asked that a couple of days ago," he said. "I can't remember anything these days."

We crossed St. Clair, the streetcar tracks gleamed in the light, and then we curled up a dark, opulent street, the houses well back from the road. The lawns were quiet and trimmed; moist, well-tended gardens, graceful columns, dew on the dark hoods of foreign cars. I was thinking to myself how extraordinary it was we ever lived here, in these fabulous houses.

We passed under the yellow clock-tower of our old school. And then slowly the car crawled up Dunvegan Road, I could see the city in the rear-view mirror, it flickered like Christmas lights all the way down to the black water. Boots scrunching in the snow, Harrow and I had stood on this hill years before, we had surveyed the whole city that lay before us, a frozen, glittering perfect jewel, an enormous playground, full of kind attentive adults, full of houses like our parents', full of mystery and pretty girls and scented living rooms and thick carpets and the smell of potpourri in the foyer. The car glided over the top of the hill and then started down the other side, circled a dark, oval park and came to a stop in front of a giant brown house. Harrow got out. So did I. We stood at the foot of the driveway.

"That was my sister's bedroom," he said.

A bell of sadness hung over him.

"Who owns it now?" I asked. But he didn't hear. He was somewhere else. I leant against the car. He looked up at the window, concentrating, as if he were trying to summon up something, as if, I imagined, he was trying to materialize behind those leaded windows and make the last twenty years vanish like a gloomy thought conceived in the passage down a hall or the turning of a corner. The window would fly open and I'd be there and we'd head off to school. The rest, that was rich food just before bed. The driver stared straight ahead. I pulled a mickey from my bag.

"Do you want a nip?" I said.

"A what?" said Harrow.

"Scotch," I said. "A little . . . " I almost said goodbye drink but I stopped myself.

He shook his head. "Maybe later." It was for my benefit he said that.

"Help yourself," he said. We got back in the car and headed downtown; the road was wet-slicked.

"It's a clean city," he said, "a hell of a clean city."

After a while he said, "You know, I think when I get to Rio I'm going to open up a little club. I'll call it the Panama Club."

"Yeah," I said, "that'd be great."

The dark car turned on to the lakeshore highway. The lake spread out black on our left. The pillars of a bridge raced by like broken teeth. Harrow looked out at the lake and laughed softly. "Maybe not," he said. "Maybe not."

We pulled away from the city; it cast up a blue glow; on the horizon a small red fan opened, blood red.

"It's starting," he said. We raced through the cool summer air.

"You got the tickets?"

He nodded but he didn't want to be distracted, not by that stuff, not now. In the rear-view mirror he watched the CN Tower flicker off and on.

"Who was your girlfriend when they built that tower, the one you used to wait for and watch the helicopter fly back and forth? The South African."

"Georgina."

"Georgina," he repeated softly. "I liked her. Whatever happened to her?"

"She went back to South Africa," I said.

The car raced through the fading night.

"I liked that story, always did. You standing in the hotel room, waiting for her to come and watching the helicopter buzz around the tower."

"Like a mosquito," I said.

"Like a mosquito."

"She wrote a book."

"Is that right?"

He opened his window and warm air rushed into the car. He wound it up again. A trumpet sighed in the background.

"I like jazz," he said. "Never understood why I don't listen to it more. I should. Maybe I will now." But that too fell back on itself.

"Like that guy in the book who says he's going to read Shakespeare every day, two hours a day, from now on, right after he stops drinking."

"Yeah. Right."

We'd had this conversation before. It was comforting to have it again. In the rear-view mirror, the red fan opened wider.

Chet Baker sang:

If I forgot to eat and sleep and pray,
Blame it on my youth.

A little sadness caught up to Harrow, like a bird outside the window. But I could feel him push it away.

"The first time my mother saw you on television I don't think she quite believed it was happening. Same name, same face, had to be a different guy. *Had* to be." A gas station, lit up but empty, flashed by.

"She's not as awful as you think, you know. She's just . . . "

"I know."

"Yeah?"

"Yeah."

"But I'll tell you one thing," he said with sudden animation. "She spent altogether too much time on you."

"How's Dorian?"

"Good," he said automatically. Then he thought about it for a minute. "She's pregnant."

"That's lovely."

"They say it skips a generation," by which he meant, I think, that his mother was going to raise the child.

"That's what they say."

"Blame it on my youth," Chet Baker sang.

The trumpet cut in.

"He never practised, this guy," Harrow said. "Never."

We drove on in silence.

It was a pale morning now. The car slowed down and wound into the airport complex. Light poured down from overhead lights. It was a sick yellow light, it passed over Harrow's face like God's judgment. He looked jaundiced.

"I hope it doesn't rain," he said. "Rain depresses me." The absurdity of what he'd just said caught up to him. He shook his head numbly. We came to a stop on the departure level. Everything fraught with meaning. But it was cheerful up there; travellers up early, hair still wet, scrubbed and packed and nervous and chattering and frowning all at once. The driver pulled out the suitcases. Harrow tipped him well, wrinkled his brow and said goodbye. The car pulled away. We went into the airport. It was blindingly lit inside. A sunny little melody floated through the air. A Pakistani family, children in their parents' arms, walked slowly by. Then a team of blue-suited stewardesses. A giant vacuum cleaner spun on a dime and headed back down the lobby.

The ticket counter was just opening up. Harrow said very quietly, "When you ask for the tickets, ask for them under the name of Jones. Say your secretary fucked up and must have ordered them under her own name."

Harrow put on his sunglasses. He turned two black-bug eyes toward me.

"I'm not sure that's a terrific idea," I said, indicating his glasses.

"Why not?"

"Because you look like you killed someone."

I couldn't tell if that landed well; the glasses were impenetrable.

"I did," he said.

At that moment, a pair of police officers walked up the centre of the room. You could tell by their gait that they were only on patrol. Under their starched brown shirts you could see the outline of bulletproof vests. Harrow took off his glasses. His eyes were pointed in my direction but they saw nothing.

"Tell me something," he said through his teeth. But I couldn't think of anything. I was frozen. It just occurred to me what I was doing, that I was aiding and abetting a felon. That if I were caught . . .

"Excuse me," I said to one of the officers. They both looked over.

"There's some confusion here. I heard the duty-free was on this floor."

"It is," the taller one said. He pointed down the hall.

"Right down there, buddy." They both had those funny rural accents that cops get.

"Is it open?"

He looked to his partner.

"I don't know."

"Like hell you don't," the other said.

He looked at me again.

"Haven't I seen you on television?"

"You have indeed."

"Fashion TV, something like that?"

"Yeah."

They moved on.

I moved my face close to Harrow's. He was frowning, his lips pursed, as if he were concentrating very hard on a math problem.

"That's so we don't have to poop in our pants every time they walk by," I said.

"You're a good man," he said meaninglessly.

I bought the tickets, paid for them in cash. Two tickets for Port of Spain, Trinidad, for the Blackwood brothers, Christian and Carl. Just the notion that we had them, that the danger with the police was past, that we had our boarding cards, gave Harrow, both of us, a little boost. We walked quickly into the cafeteria.

"What's Dizzy Gillespie like?" he asked.

"Dead," I said.

"Who's the world's biggest asshole?"

"That's easy. Ziggy Marley. Just an impossible little coon."

I meant to catch him off guard, to make him laugh, but I caught, out of the corner of my eye, a tiny splinter of sadness catch him in the heart. I think he was sorry he'd asked, that the conversation had taken this direction. Suddenly his own life must have stood up among the confetti and flashbulbs and fan magazines, and its sheer appallingness filled him with nausea. Something sank in my stomach. I shouldn't have gone on so gleefully. I should have cooled it. It was an illness: I'd flushed with pleasure when the cop recognized me. I was even happy for Harrow to have seen it. All my life I'd wanted to beat him, to whip him, but it gave me no pleasure now. None. But Harrow was firing all four pistons today, like a man who's just woken up sober, and he wasn't going to get all leaden and sad. It'd get in the way.

"How about Leonard Cohen?" he said.

"Well, I never got to meet him, did I?"

We sat at the far end of the cafeteria, Harrow with his back to the room. I went and got the coffees, orange juice and a pair of Danishes. I was dying for a belt. Canned Beatle music played in the background.

"I wonder if they had any idea that thirty years down the road this song was going to end up in an airport at six o'clock in the morning. It must have been unimaginable," Harrow said. He was pulling himself up. It was an effort but his feet were leaving the mud.

"Where do you want to stay in Port of Spain?" he said. And then didn't wait for the answer. "Let's stay somewhere nice. I'm going to be pooped. I want to get this thing off on the right foot." A pause. "We'll get to town, we'll get a bottle of Russian vodka, we'll get a nice room. It'll be fine. I've got until Monday morning till they know I'm gone. Surely we can get out of town by then." He laughed exuberantly.

A group of kids waiting for a flight to Acapulco burst into the cafeteria. Tennis rackets, loud shirts, young office girls in too much make-up, their weight-lifting boyfriends, everybody wide-awake and ready for a holiday.

"I think we're going to the wrong party," Harrow said to a young girl at the next table. Her boyfriend checked him out quickly, then pretended to lose interest. I wanted her to like Harrow, to banter a bit with him, but there must have been something about his early-morning energy, a certain kind of energy, that put her off. Harrow extracted his sunglasses from a breast pocket and snapped them on. He was looking for mischief now. He turned two giant sunglassed bulbs to me, he looked like an insect, and said, for the young girl's benefit, "What we need is erotica, not pornography."

She didn't get it but, a few tables over, a black man tittered.

Outside it was daylight. A plane took off. You could see it rise slowly off the tarmac and head up into the early-morning blue sky.

We followed soon after, the shadow of the plane passing over a green field. We did a slow bank and moved out over water. A small white sailboat ran along the shoreline. The plane dropped in an air pocket. Convulsively I grabbed the armrest. I looked at the stewardess, at the passengers beside me, at a man with red hair who sat in front of me. Is this how people look who are just about to die? The plane rose up and up and up and then a bell sounded, someone lit a cigarette, the smoke drifted down the aisle.

I was going to order a Bloody Mary but I didn't want Harrow to feel more alone than he did, so I left it.

"When we get to the hotel," he said, "we'll get a bucket of ice, lock the door, let the breeze blow in the window and then I'll have a drink with you." He opened a book of Walt Whitman and read for a moment.

"Did Tom Murphy say anything about me?" he asked.

"He was too full of loathing for me. It distracted him." He nodded and went back to his green book. Like gravity, it was catching up to him again.

Sometime soon after breakfast was served. A Spanish omelet which was delicious. I watched Harrow wolf his food down. He held his spoon like a child, in a fist, as if someone were going to try and take it away. I'd forgotten. He had terrible table manners. They all did. For a woman so consumed with appearances, it always amazed me Florence Winncup let her kids out of the kennel with those manners.

"He seemed disgusted by the proceedings," Harrow said, wiping his mouth.

"Tom?"

"Yes. As if, out of duty, he'd attend, but this stuff was definitely beneath him."

"Harrow," I said, "Tom Murphy is an asshole."

"Yeah?"

"I'm sure he's *delighted* by the turn of events."

He thought for a second.

"Boy, that's a hard row to hoe."

He caught a passing stewardess's eye. In fact he threw up his hand like a pupil.

"May I have an orange juice, please?" he said. She nodded coldly.

"I wonder what I could have done to alienate her," he said. Everything bruised him now.

After a moment: "How come they speak Portuguese in Brazil? That doesn't make any sense at all."

"The point is, Harrow, Tom Murphy could have been a little bit more generous."

"Exactly," he said, not looking up, holding on to another thought. But he didn't express it. His face softened and it was gone. He was reading again.

The plane sailed high, high up over the water. The bar service rattled by.

"You know that apartment we had on McMaster Street?" I asked.

He leaned his ear toward me, staring straight ahead, as if what he was about to hear might be important.

"Yeah?" he said uncertainly.

"You know, the one a bit up Avenue Road?"

"Yeah, yeah."

"I went back there last week." After a pause. "Do you ever do that? Go back to those old places, old houses, old apartments?"

He thought for a moment.

"No, I don't," he said politely. "I know you do, but I don't."

"They've got screens over the windows now."

He nodded sombrely, thoughtfully, he was trying to get a fix on it, on what I was talking about, about why it might be important, even worth mentioning, but he couldn't, he simply couldn't, and suddenly the laughter poured out of him like beans from a ripped bag. He bent over his breakfast, his shoulders shaking soundlessly.

"I'm sorry. I'm not good at this stuff," he said. "It must be hysterics."

"Important stuff," I said. "Someone's got to notice."

He wiped away the tears. "Of course they do."

A woman with a baby in her arms walked slowly down the aisle. She looked exhausted.

Lunch came and went. There was a movie. It was stupid and poignant at the same time; there's something about flying that opens you up. I never weep at the movies except when I'm in an airplane. Up there, just about anything gets to me.

Then the lights came back on; the window panels flew up. The plane smelt stuffy, like a bedroom with someone asleep in it. I got up for a walk; people slumbered under blankets, read books, drank, talked; it was all very intimate, very cosy, even among strangers. A Chinese man did a set of exotic stretching exercises at the back of the plane. A red-faced Englishman stood by the bar, helping himself. He had a remark for everyone. Friendly and garrulous, he had that deadly staying power. I had a feeling he'd drunk to sleep several sets of companions.

"Young man," he said to me, "come here."

I kept moving, but with a smile and sure enough, by the time I'd got back to my seat, he'd corralled the father of the Pakistani family, who was too polite to disengage immediately.

"You see those scratches on the window," Harrow said. "They're on the outside. How do you suppose they got on the outside?"

The intercom clicked on. Immigration cards were handed out. It looked very strange to see Harrow sign my signature.

My ears popped. Harrow looked hopefully out the window. He was thinking about the rain again. Or that's what I thought he was thinking about.

"You know," he said after a while, "most of the people I've sucked up to have never given me fuck all."

The plane broke though the clouds. The green island fell away beneath us. The wheels touched down on the brown tarmac. There was a splatter of applause. The doors opened. Warm air rushed into the plane like children into a party. It was a beautiful, windy day. A yellow shack stood at the very edge of the runway. The sea sparkled.

"Could be worse," Harrow said cautiously. "Could be worse."

Those were the last words we said to each other until we met on the other side of customs. I went first.

"Business or pleasure?" the agent asked.

"Oh, pleasure," I said, and shut my mouth. It was an effort. I had a terrible desire to talk, to make him my best friend. I didn't look back, I put my passport in my breast pocket and then I was through.

There's nothing quite like the smell of an airport in the tropics: hot cement, jet fumes, blond tobacco and warm bodies. I stopped in a gift shop and bought a book on local vegetation. Even though I knew it was inappropriate, I felt some kind of excited happiness, and relief, I guess, relief that life did something *other* than just plod on, that there still existed moments when it pressed hard against you, and left its marks, vivid and indelible. I was going to remember this day, it was going to stand out, not like the day before or the week before: All that was like a column of dusty soldiers marching wearily past.

I went outside. In the distance trees bent in the wind. A black cab pulled up beside me in the airport and I got in. Harrow was in the back. We pulled away, following the shoreline into town. The traffic was bad; lorries sputtered coughs of lead-blue fumes. It took an hour to go twenty miles. Soca music bounced from the radio. The driver asked us if we wanted a couple of beers. I said not now. While white flowers bobbed in the wind in front of Harrow's childhood house in Forest Hill, the black cab drove through Port of Spain, white and yellow buildings, the street teeming, busy, hot. We climbed a sharp hill.

It was a strange hotel, built into the side of a ravine, a kind of upside-down place, the lobby on the top floor, the rooms below.

"Why, it's just like hell," Harrow said. The porter carried our bags into a high-ceilinged, draughty lobby. To warm the place up, they'd put ferns and plants here and there but it didn't work; they stood alone, stringy and ignored, like unpopular girls at a dance. An Englishman read the newspaper defiantly in the lobby. A pair of elderly men practised synchronized swimming in the pool.

We took the elevator down to our room. It was orange with

double beds. I yanked open the windows. From below came the plink plink of a tennis game. We looked across an oval field where kids played soccer, where a little boy with no pants flew a kite. The kite sailed high up in the air, catching the light like a shield; behind it the ocean was dark and white-wave capped. Harrow lay down on the bed.

"We've got to make a plane reservation," he said. "Fuck, I'm so tired I can hardly see." He was unwinding like a clock.

"I'll do it," I said.

"I'll have to pass on that drink," he said. "I'm too pooped." He kicked his shoes off and lay on the mattress staring at the ceiling. This was the first room after his own bedroom, the first of many foreign rooms, foreign ceilings, foreign beds, foreign desks with no history saturated into the wood. It was an unthinkable thought.

"I think I'll sleep for a while," he said. I closed the curtains; the wind blew them apart in puffs. I stood in the dark room for a second.

"Harrow," I said.

But there was no answer. He had retreated into sleep. I tiptoed out into the hall. I went down into the lobby, looked in the bar, then headed out into town.

It was a boiling hot day, the sun bearing down. I made my way incuriously along the sidewalk, it was sticky on my feet. Down the road, a madman with a head shaved bald as a nut crossed the street and headed straight for me. He stooped over and picked up a stick. I fled across the street. The passersby shouted at him. Everyone knew him. A woman put her hand on my arm and told me to pay him no heed, that he was harmless. I left him there, his back to the football field, waving his stick, a crazy brown man with a bald head. I looked way up the side of the hotel. Somewhere near the top was our room. And in there Harrow slept quietly. What was he dreaming about? What would he think about when he awoke? The first alien room–now there would be others. There'd be the hotel in Rio, the new apartment, no friends, the lonely dinners, the problems with a new language. I walked on through the sun-baked town. A naked, dusty man lay in a doorway, his cock flopped like a banana on the sidewalk.

I stepped over him. I passed a yellow building. It was a prison. Now that I was here, now what? Now that Harrow was here, now what? What do you do in a foreign country? Read books, wait for meals, what else? Hot countries are a graveyard for white people. I felt a wave of urgency, as if I should be there when Harrow awoke. I turned around and walked briskly back to the hotel. I was in a full sweat when I arrived. I stepped into the ice-cold lobby and went back down to the room. I opened the door.

"Harrow," I said. There was no answer. "Harrow," I said. Still nothing. I waited a second. The air conditioning fell silent. I listened and I listened. I could hear breathing; and then, against the blue sea, in a crack in the curtains, his blankets rose up and down and up and down. A man couldn't stop breathing even if he wanted to. I went to the bar and had a drink by myself. I stared out to sea. I borrowed the phone. I made a plane reservation for Christian Blackwood to fly the following morning to Caracas and then on to Rio. I booked it under my name. He could change it when he picked up the ticket. "My secretary fucked up." I could hear him say it, see him say it, his forehead wrinkled, a Forest Hill smile on his face. It was like a mother tongue, that face, his mother had taught it to him and now he'd never be free of it.

It was a twelve-hour flight to Rio, all in all. All this would seem like a drunken flash by the time he arrived there.

It got dark. The bar filled with couples, then a family from Chicago. I wanted company, but I could see they were having a holiday together, it was their time and I left them alone. I had another drink. Then another. Sometime after eight I went back up to Harrow's room and tried to wake him up. He didn't answer. I sat down beside his bed. I turned on the light. He rolled over. He put his hands behind his head.

"Jesus," he said, and in a tone of voice that broke my heart. "I was just having quite the dream."

I imagine he was. I wanted him to get up. I'd seen a pink

restaurant down the road, it looked rather cheerful, rather fun, and I hoped we could have dinner there. Goat and lots of booze. Get really pissed up and stagger into town and have a night of it. But that wasn't for him. He lay there for a second, got up, wrapped himself in a sheet–he was oddly modest about that, I think he was embarrassed now about his weight–took a pee, I heard the toilet seat crash down and then he came back in the room.

"I think I'm going to go back to bed," he said. "I'm beat." It was selfish but I felt a grain of disappointment.

"Maybe some food would do you good," I said.

"Nothing would do me any good."

It was the closest to self-pity he came that whole trip. I left him in the room.

"Do you want the light out?" I said.

It reminded me of something that you might say to a lover when you creep from her bed at 5:30 in the morning.

"Please," he said and I heard him roll over. I went back to the bar. I had another drink. I stared out at the huge ocean swells and I daydreamed about Harrow and me, I daydreamed we were little kids and we were out there on those high, rolling waves; we were in a freighter and we were headed off to a country full of jungles and snakes and Indians with spears.

I don't remember going back to my room that night, I must have been pretty drunk. I turned on the television but I can't recall what I watched. At six in the morning the lobby phoned with a wake-up call. I couldn't remember having told them to but I was glad they did. I had a giddy, sickening hangover but the import of that morning, those few hours, drove it backwards, at least for a while. We ordered room service. I drank a quart of orange juice. And then, when the curtains blew apart and sun came in and a plane flew overhead and a man jogged around the playing field below the window, suddenly it was time to go. I went to the lobby with him. We looked at each other in the elevator. It was hard to turn away. Harrow took a couple of deep inhalations as though he were trying to connect his body to where he was. And then we were in that cold lobby again. I stopped at the desk, told the woman I'd be staying for another day, then went outside into the white-hot sunshine with Harrow. Bougainvillea blossomed on the side of the hotel. A chauffeured limo drove up, the driver hopped out and took Harrow's bags. I wrapped my arms around him. "I love you," I said.

"I love you too," he said and then kissed me on the cheek. He got in the cab. He wound down the window. He wiped his brow.

"It's a hot one," he said, and then the car pulled away. I saw a hand wave in the back black window; the car rolled down the hill and then disappeared behind the beautiful plants.

Chapter Fourteen

In television, they always forgive you if they can't replace you. There was a bit of sulking when I went in the next day. An Irish executive producer called me into his office and after a round of cordial small talk told me "this must never happen again." I said I'd forgotten, gone away to visit a friend. He paused when I said that. Being Irish he must have figured I went on a binge and was lying about it.

Anyway, in the weeks that followed, I befriended the host of the show. He was a long-faced New Zealander with hennaed hair. I liked him. He was bright and very amusing but terribly vain and I realized I could use that. One day he confided to me that he wanted to write a novel. I took him out for a drink that evening and in a dark bar I made the observation that by the time Scott Fitzgerald was his age, he had already written three novels, including *The Great Gatsby*. I don't know if that tipped the scales, but a couple of weeks later he quit. There was a hurried search, the Irishman asked me if I was interested, I said no, absolutely not, and that cinched it. How odd it was that the ripples from Harrow's misfortune, an authentic tragedy, continued to enrich my life. It had changed everything.

I got a letter from Thailand. He was moving around. A couple of weeks later I got another letter. It was suicidal. I think he was in his cups, sitting on a beach somewhere, the sun setting, couples walking by together, salsa music drifting over the sand and the water, a savage red sky, and, like a child who's been keeping it in all day, he just let go of it in the letter.

Near the end of November, the show sent me over to England to interview George Harrison. He'd just made a new album and I was going to talk to him in his office in London. It seemed like kind of a crowning moment, going to meet a Beatle. But I fussed and fussed. What should I ask him first? It's the first question that sets the tone for an interview, lets them know you're not an asshole.

"George, are you concerned that since the death of John, there's someone out there saying 'And now there are three?'"

No, perhaps not. Not the first question.

Kalie drove me to the airport in the morning. It was a cold blue day with a wind still smelling of winter blowing up from the lake and slapping you across the face. The sunlight hurt my eyes and I was nervous about the plane. I figured I was too happy these days, that I was going to die. It made a kind of sense. The night before, when I stripped down the little boy for his tub, I put his T-shirt in my suitcase. It smelt like him; it'd be good luck.

"Do I look lucky to you?" I said to Kalie.

She was wearing a baseball jacket with *Prairie Hill Cowboys* on the back.

"Yes," she said, "you've got horseshoes up your bum these days."

That didn't settle my doubts.

"I feel like I'm going to be punished for something," I said.

Kalie wound her dirty blue car up on to the four-lane highway going to the airport.

"Do you feel unlucky?" she asked. But I didn't answer. I was imagining, instead, a very complicated cartoon of thousands and thousands of beads, all different colours, all streaming through a glass tube toward the airport. They were green and blue and orange and purple, but there were red ones too; they were the ones who were going to die that day in a plane crash. As we got closer to the airport the blue beads fell away, then the green, then the black, then the mauve, the yellow, the orange, the pink, until there was only a red stream pouring through a funnel into the departure lobby.

I tried to explain it to Kalie. She listened patiently. We drove on in silence, and she eased the car off the highway and on to a ramp and then glided slowly up a rise into the terminal. She pulled the car over.

"And you figure you're one of the red beads?" she said.

"Exactly." A car honked behind her. She kissed me on the cheek.

"Don't forget to get his autograph," she said. "And get it on *Beatlemania*, one of the early records. Not that later stuff."

I thought about Harrow on the plane going over. It was one of those memories that pop out of nowhere, you can't tell where it came from. I must have been thirteen or fourteen. I was wandering through our school one afternoon after everyone had gone home. It was winter. Darkness fell. Ghostly figures passed quickly on the streets outside. I could hear the janitor moving up the hall, the clank of the bucket. I was fishing around in the teacher's desk, looking for chalk to play on the board with, when I came across a stack of cards. My hands shook when I realized what they were. They were comment cards; bits of advice, private observations from our teacher the year before. I flipped through them. I recognized this name then that name. I looked for mine. It was near the beginning, right before Brinkley. Yes, there it was: Blackwood, Christian. I looked at the words written underneath: *Unbelievably childish.*

Nothing more. Now I know that childhood is a time for blows to the heart and the vanity, but this packed a wallop. It made my knees shake. What made it so devastating was that the teacher had appeared to adore me, to find me funny and arresting. I had preened in his presence, been at my very best And now this: *Unbelievably childish.*

He must have been in a bad mood, I thought, a very bad mood indeed when he filled out my card. I flipped to the back of the stack to see what he'd said about Harrow. If he was wrong about me, he'd be wrong about Harrow.

It was the last card in the deck and it read: *A sterling individual. Conscientious, clever, decent, a real find. We can expect great things from this lad!* We all rearrange the world so that we come out near the top, it's a natural muscular reflex, but this required effort. After a half-hour or so, on the way home, I figured it out. He must have done our cards at different times. Mine when he was sour; Harrow's later, when he was feeling better.

I had a feeling, up there in the airplane, feeling sorry for myself the way you do when you're very happy, that Harrow's life, wherever it was, wasn't so bad. I imagined he was in the centre of some admiring small expatriate group somewhere who'd met this "amazing Walt Whitman–loving lawyer who killed a guy." It would make him a kind of star, a romantic figure. I allowed myself to see Harrow's life unfolding like a novel. I'd talked about it so much that it was beginning to seem just like that, a story. I had lost touch somewhere with the real Harrow, a radiant child grown prematurely old.

I got to London, I still hadn't figured out that first question.

"George, there are those who say that there is only one war in literature and that is the Trojan war. Does the same principle hold true for music and, if so, what is that song?"

No. No, no.

I checked into a big cold hotel where I heard a violin cover of "Can't Buy Me Love" in the elevator. It seemed like a good sign.

I thought a lot about Harrow that weekend in London. I don't know why, perhaps because I was travelling and so was he and it gave me just a taste of what his life must be like, all those foreign ceilings you look up at.

Anyway, when the morning came for the interview I was nervous as a cat. *"George, Tennessee Williams was a playwright who continued writing long after his best work. Is there a time when it is the artist's responsibility to say 'That's enough. I'm done'?"*

The cab driver talked too much. He shattered my concentration. "There's MI6, counter-intelligence," he said, driving slowly around a stone grey building. I didn't reply. But he didn't notice. He was still talking when I walked away from the cab.

I went into a brownstone building and up to the third floor. The crew was there, two cameras, a blaze of lights, two soundmen, a producer, an assistant, a secretary from the bureau; everyone very thrilled, just waiting. That's when I heard it, that Liverpool accent, right behind me, in the doorway.

"Oh," it said, "you're here already. I didn't think it was television, I thought it was radio."

I turned around and there he was: lanky, sinewy, dark hair pushed behind his ears, a lined, lived-in face, big teeth.

"I should brush my hair."

"I'm Christian Blackwood," I said.

"I'm George Harrison," he said.

I couldn't get over that accent, that voice. I went back over to the window and took a deep breath. I looked out again. It was grey and overcast. I looked down the street; a man with a scarf around his neck was talking with great animation. Beside him, a small blond woman, her hair up in a bun, listened severely.

"We're ready over here," the producer said.

Harrison drummed on the arm of his chair and looked up pleasantly.

I sat down, smiled.

Was that Harrow? Could it have been him? Why here? Why London? Is he following me?

"So George," I began, my mind wiped clean as an after-school blackboard, "what was it like being in the Beatles?"

The room sagged. The producer looked paralysed with dismay. Even the cameraman, trained like a pointer, flinched. Harrison paused. He looked away, thinking of an answer. Determined to take the question seriously and, with it, the person who asked it.

"Well, you know, for a first job it wasn't too bad."

Everyone relaxed. With a guy like that, you can't go wrong.

Chapter Fifteen

I don't want to make too much of it, but the business with Harrow changed me. After that trip to Trinidad, something fell off me, like a bumper off an aging car. And, oddly enough, it took me a long time even to notice. One night, years later, I was dropping Jesse off at a birthday party. His best friend had just turned twelve, and there were girls and music at a house up on Dunvegan Road, just down the street from Harrow Winncup's old house. We pulled to a stop. An athletic, excitable boy jumped out and set off across the lawn with only a little wave backwards. He could hardly wait to get inside.

"Jesse," I called from the car, "are you coming back to my house or your mother's after?"

"Whichever," he said cheerfully.

I followed him all the way to the door, watched him knock. A boy with two girls behind him opened the door. The girls cheered, the boy pounded him on the back. The excitement of young voices at the beginning of a party spilled out across the quiet street and then the door closed and they were gone. The house and time had swallowed them up.

I sat there for a few moments longer and then I looked around. I realized where I was. I hadn't been there for ages, not since that morning, that long, slow, sad drive to the airport with Harrow.

I must have been cured, without even knowing it, of my nostalgia, of a constant hunger for old houses and schools, the need to feel the stirring of ghosts. There was a staleness in their presence now, I could feel it, a stirring that promised action, that keyed the nervous system to the arrival of something that was never going to arrive again. No voices, no cries, no children with their shirttails out would ever again run breathlessly down those streets toward me. Like the boy in the window, they were gone forever. It wasn't tragic or even sad but I realized, sitting in my car that early evening, that I had long since ceased to seek out the things that had once impressed themselves so deeply on me. Now I left them alone.

I got a few more letters from Harrow–odd I can't remember how many–but then they sort of dried up and I stopped looking for them.

His mother made a deal on the arson charge; claimed her doctor had overprescribed tranquilizers; they had produced a state of "involuntary intoxication" during which she had set fire to her store. She got a letter from a psychiatrist, made full restitution, and the whole affair just blew quietly away.

Harrow came home a couple of years later. I read about it in the newspaper. He didn't get in touch with me, and it didn't surprise me. They arrested him at the airport; he went to trial, was found guilty of manslaughter, did eight months in a minimum-security prison.

I ran into my cousin Warren a little while ago. He was on his way to an AA meeting. I didn't ask about Harrow but he brought his name up anyway.

"Did you hear the news?" he said. "Harrow's been re-instated."

I didn't follow.

"To the law board. He can practise again."

Warren shook his head with admiration. "What a guy eh? Eh?"

In fact, since then, I've heard from a couple of people that Harrow plans to appeal his conviction, see if he can get it quashed. He says the crown covered up some key evidence. It may work too, who knows? I've heard of stranger things.

As for him and me, we're finished. There are some things you can't go back from and there was a little bit too much damage on both sides to make it worth picking it up again. It's not anger. I think that in this life Harrow and I have just about had enough of each other. But it's true about old friends: when they fall out of your life, it's like losing a tooth. It just leaves a blank. You never fill it again.

I did see him again though, only once. I was sitting in a restaurant when I caught sight of him down the street. He was coming this way, looking in store windows. He looked lean, he must have stopped drinking, and his hair was wild, knotted in a ponytail I didn't like. Just as he came abreast of the window a woman I didn't know started talking to me. I half turned in my seat to listen. Out of the corner of my eye I saw Harrow stop and turn square to the window, pause a second. I could feel his face widen into a smile, there was a moment's hesitation and then he was gone.